GIFTED TO THE FROST KING

A MONSTROUS HOLIDAY SERIES

BOOK 1

CHARLOTTE SWAN

Copyright © 2024 by Charlotte Swan

eBook ISBN: 978-1-960615-09-1

Cover Design by Charlotte Swan

www.authorcharlotteswan.com

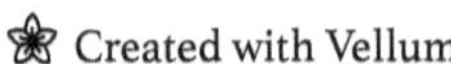 Created with Vellum

For a list of content and trigger warnings please check the author's website.

authorcharlotteswan.com

For anyone who's ever thought, what if Jack Frost was a cursed elf king with a filthy mouth...

1

———

DOVE

My old boot crunches through the thick layer of snow as I try to free one last carrot from the frozen ground.

Gripping the green stem in my gloved hand, I brace myself and pull hard. The carrot breaks through the ice with a resounding crack, and I nearly fall on my backside. It wouldn't matter much if I did. I'm already soaked to the bone from the icy wind. My toes went numb an hour ago. My wool socks are squishy—wet from the hole in the toe that still desperately needs mending.

Mama has had much on her plate recently, and I haven't had the heart to add fixing my worn boots to it.

Therefore, I grit my teeth against the blistering cold, push my discomfort from my mind, and toss the last meager carrot into my fraying basket. Five carrots and two potatoes is a meager haul. I can only hope my sister has had more luck. Glancing across the snowy field, my eyes land on Sophia's small frame as she fights with her own stubborn vegetable.

My sister's long scarf whips in the wind. Snow settles on her coat-covered shoulders. Tendrils of her dark hair cling to her pink cheeks. Glancing towards the sky, I sigh as the thick white clouds roll overhead. The dusting we are getting is about to take a turn for the worst.

The scent of fresh cinnamon bread tickles my nose. I drop my gaze down towards our cottage. Smoke billows from the crumbling chimney and orange light beams through the two front-facing windows. My stomach growls, reminding me I haven't eaten today.

Tucking my basket in the crook of my arm, I cup my hands around my mouth.

"Sophia!" I call, watching her turn towards me. "Come. Let's head inside before you turn into an icicle."

She picks up her basket and stomps over to me—the deep snow rising nearly to her knees. The skirt of her wool dress is sodden. Once she is next to me, I take in her shivering body. Before we head inside, we must commence with our usual ritual.

"Two potatoes and four carrots," she says proudly, holding up her basket.

Her scarf is wrapped around the lower part of her face, muffling her soft voice. Her blue eyes sparkle with pride. She, Mama, and I all share the same dark hair, but only Sophia was blessed with Papa's light eyes. Whenever I look at her, warm memories of him flood me.

Smirking down at her, my cheeks sting from wind-burn.

"Two potatoes," I say, raising my basket in triumph. "And *five* carrots."

Her dark brows pull down, and I know she's frowning even with her mouth covered. Her small hand tips my basket as she peers inside.

"No fair," she huffs. "Mine are bigger!"

"The game has always been about quantity—not size." I wave a dismissive hand.

Sophia pouts as she sets off towards the house. The numbness in my toes has now spread to my whole foot. Unsticking my legs, I trudge along after her.

The game helps Sophia see this chore as something fun, even if the task is dreadful. Papa used to play it with me, showering me with praise when my hauls were bigger than his. Those were the days when our harvests were much more significant: ten potatoes instead of four, fifteen carrots instead of nine.

Ever since Sophia was born ten years ago, and we lost Papa to illness in the months following her birth, the weather in our small town of Snowdale has gotten worse. I fear Sophia will only know hardship if it persists. The snow and ice have to let up. We won't survive much longer if our bounties continue to be this meager.

That is why tomorrow is so important.

I quickly catch up to Sophia, and we huddle under our wet coats to share body heat. Sophia is quiet as we walk—lost in her thoughts as always. I don't mind the silence, especially when each deep breath shreds my lungs with icy claws.

We make it to the front door of our cottage just as the wind picks up. Kicking the snow off our boots, we enter our home and latch the creaking door. Sophia and I hang our wet coats and mittens on the pegs near the door before taking off our shoes. Bright orange flames snap and flicker in the hearth. The heat lures Sophia and I towards it. The warmth licks over my cold cheeks and returns feeling back in my hands.

The oven door slams shut and I glance towards our tiny kitchen. Mama rises from her crouched position with a fresh loaf of cinnamon bread. She was able to barter for the elusive spice in the market a few weeks ago, and I've been patiently waiting for her to make it ever since.

It's not surprising she chose today.

Flour decorates the front of her simple, dark gown. Gray hair curls around her temples, and her dark eyes glow warmly as she takes us in. She smiles, and the wrinkles around her mouth stretch with the movement. It's warm, if a little brittle—the weight of tomorrow lingers between us in the cottage.

Picking up our baskets, I set them down next to her on the counter.

"Four potatoes and nine carrots. Sophia found the most."

My sister turns from her place at the fire with wide blue eyes. I send her a quick wink and am rewarded with her toothy grin. Mama goes through our baskets, sifting through each vegetable.

"Thank you, girls. These will do well in a stew. We still have some meat from the butcher." Her eyes roam over my face. "We should eat the last of it tonight."

"Mama," I say, reaching for her hand.

Her slender fingers come down on top of mine in a reassuring squeeze.

"I just never thought this day would come," she whispers, shaking her head.

I glance at Sophia, who's too busy warming her toes by the fire to hear us. I'll never forget having to explain to her what tomorrow was. As much as we all pretended it wasn't happening, we knew from the moment I turned twenty-five, it was a matter of if not when I'd be sent out into the snow and offered to *him*.

By being unmarried and childless at what our town deems an old age, I am forced to submit for *the Offering*. It is the price I must pay if I wish for myself and my family to remain in Snowdale. There are stories about the families who don't comply—how they were turned out of their homes by a mob and left to freeze out in the barren, icy wastelands surrounding our town.

My eyes linger on Sophia a moment longer. With our age difference, many would expect us not to be close. Even more would believe I should already be married with at least one child of my own. I knew at fifteen my life plan wouldn't look like many of the other young women around me.

With Papa gone and Sophia still a baby, Mama needed my help raising her. We have spent every day together—working together and loving each other fiercely. The three of us rely on each other for everything, and that's why—no matter how barbaric I think this ritual is—I will partake without fuss to keep them safe.

I wouldn't be opposed to a family of my own, but as we live in one of the most remote cottages, our trips into town are sparse. Besides, it's not as if Snowdale is brimming with eligible suitors. We rarely get travelers passing through, and the ones we do are frost-bitten old men.

Marrying Jon would've taken me out of contention for tomorrow, but I'd rather swallow a kitchen knife than be his bride.

He is one of the only men in our village who has ever paid me much attention—unwelcome as it is. Our last interaction still burns in the back of my mind. Jon had caught me on my way home from the market. Cornering me against an old barn with his breath reeking of ale, he declared his intention to put forth an offer of marriage to my mother. Stating with a smug sneer, he knew how much we could use the coin.

I can still recall his gloved hand sliding over my cheek and his coat opening to show the ornately carved handle of the knife strapped to his hip. Looking for a way out of the conversation, I had told him I was going through with *the Offering;* my deadline to be married and avoid it had already passed.

"Hmm," he had purred against my ear. "*The Offering* is a simple delay. Once it is over, I will have you. I take it you are familiar with my reputation?"

I had nodded reluctantly—the stories of his cruelty and brutality were well-known. A smile graced his cracked lips, exposing two rows of yellowed teeth.

"Good. Then you should know I always get what I want." His beady eyes ran down the length of my body as if he was looking at me unclothed. "Using a little force is something I've never shied away from."

Bile swam up my throat then, just as it does now. A man like Jon Nine-Fingers—a nickname he claims was bestowed on him while doing something heroic, but everyone in Snowdale knows he lost his thumb during a bar fight—would trap me in a marriage of pain and misery. The thought of bearing his children makes my stomach turn.

I allow the roaring fire to melt away the remnants of the icy memory. Mama squeezes my hand once more before I drop hers. She stares at me another moment, eyes rimming with red. The sight of her tears encourages my own to form.

We share a soft smile before she shakes herself and wipes her palms on her skirt.

"Why don't you two change out of those wet clothes, and I'll get started on supper."

Sophia and I head to the bedroom, and I help her out of her wet gown. Even her shift and wool socks are soaked. There must be a hole in her coat somewhere. If I can find our old needle and thread, I'll try to patch it for her. Slipping a fresh, dry nightgown over her head, I unbraid her soft hair knowing it will dry faster unbound.

"Thank you, Dove," she says, kissing my cheek before setting off for the table.

Our cottage is small; Mama sleeps in a loft above the main room while Sophia and I share a bed behind a curtain just off the front room. I love my mother and my sister—I'd happily spend my life with them, but this constant existence of working hard for mere scraps is no life.

What kind of future will Sophia have? How can I start a family when their future is nothing but hardship? What will it be like for Sophia's children?

We'll be lucky if this cottage survives until Sophia becomes an adult—I doubt there will be anything left to inherit by the time she gets married. The roof leaks, a draft trickles in from every window, and the floorboards have started rotting from the snow.

Things have to change—I believe they will somehow. I have to, or else I would never get out of bed. Even if change in Snowdale seems as impossible as a day without snow.

Sitting on the creaking bed, I peel off my wet stockings, knowing they'll need to be set before the fire. I untie the laces at the back of my gown until the fabric gapes. I rise slowly to my feet. The material hits the wooden floor with a wet thud. Stepping out of it, I inspect my toes, happy to see no traces of frostbite.

I slide off my wet shift and put on an old nightgown and fresh wool socks. Bundling up in a thick robe, I pad out to the main room and take my usual spot at the kitchen table. Mama ladles thick brown stew into our bowls. Steam curls over the lip of the cracked ceramic, and I lower my face to absorb the warmth.

My stomach growls as Mama slices off thick pieces of cinnamon bread. The sweet scent invades my lungs.

"If only we had butter," Mama says softly, shaking her head.

"You know I've always preferred it plain."

She smiles softly at me and sets a slice on my plate—the cinnamon and sugar swirl throughout the pale-colored bread. The crust is a perfect golden brown. Somehow, Mama always manages to turn frostbitten scraps into a delicious meal. The meat in our stew is a bad cut, tough and inedible most of the time, but Mama has a way of making it unbelievably tender.

Sophia picks up her spoon, a large chunk of potatoes resting on it, and brings it towards her mouth. Mama clears her throat and casts a pointed look.

"Sophia, you know what we must do before we eat."

Pursing her lips, Sophia returns her spoon to the bowl with a soft clank.

"Sorry, Mama," she sighs before bowing her head.

I follow suit.

"*Mother of the Snow*," Mama prays. "We thank you for this harvest—even in these harsh conditions, you find a way for us to survive. We thank you for our health. We pray that Nick, who was a loving father and husband, has found peace with you and is no longer in pain. I thank you for my two beautiful girls—without them, I would never have known the true meaning of love. I beg you to please look out for them and—"

Her breath catches on a sob. Both Sophia and I snap our heads up. Tears pour over her pale cheeks and collect in the hollow of her throat.

"Please," she sobs, "*please* spare my Dove tomorrow."

Reaching out, I take her hands. They are warm and as familiar as my own. Tears slip from my eyes, but I quickly wipe them away. Nothing can be done now; sadness over what's happening tomorrow won't change it. Of course, I am worried despite the history of *the Offering*.

There is always a chance he will come—finally choosing one of us to fulfill our part of whatever curse he's put upon this land. Not that I have any particular desire to be selected. One of the others up there with me tomorrow can be the chosen one—undoubtedly, one wants to be remembered as the person who stopped the snow.

A soft sniffle makes me look over. Sophia's blue eyes are red, and wetness courses down her round cheeks. Dropping Mama's hand, I push back from the table—my wooden chair scraping against the floor.

"Oh, Soph," I sigh, opening my arms. "Come here. Don't cry. Everything will be alright."

Sophia rounds the table and rushes towards me. Barreling into my arms, I hold her petite body in my lap, not liking how cold she still feels. Rubbing my arms up and down her sides, my heart pangs.

I love them—I'd never wish to leave them—but if I am chosen tomorrow, perhaps there is comfort in the fact that I will have improved their lives somehow. I don't want to be a savior, but my sacrifice wouldn't be in vain if it meant granting Sophia the future she deserves.

However, now is not the time to voice those thoughts. Besides, there's a real chance that all this worry is for nothing.

"*He* may not even come. No one's ever been chosen," I remind her.

Sophia scrunches her nose.

"Not true, Mrs. Pendleton says someone was chosen. A long time ago, *he* picked a boy and they found his bones scattered—"

"Enough, Sophia. You know Mrs. Pendleton is a dreadful lair." Mama shakes her head. "Regardless, it is a vile custom. Even if one of you is taken, how do we know that dreadful creature will keep his word? The curse was laid on this land long before any of us were born."

It is true. Whatever caused him to curse our land in the first place was not our doing, and yet we are still being punished for it. It is all dreadfully unfair, but we have no choice. I will do my duty to Snowdale and hope I don't freeze to death in the process.

"Mrs. Pendleton *is* a dreadful liar," I agree. "There's no reason to think this year is any different than all the others."

Mama nods reluctantly.

"He hasn't shown at an *Offering* since I was a little girl. I don't know whether that's a good or bad omen. If the weather is any indication, I'm inclined to believe the latter."

"No matter how poor the weather gets, at least we have each other."

Clasping my mother's hand, Sophia tightens her hold around my neck.

"Forever?" Sophia asks.

My eyes connect with Mama's—our matching eyes share our matching worry. I let my mask fall, if only for a moment. I let her see the fear in my eyes that I've shoved down so that I don't do something foolish and run away—damning my family in the process. I let her see that I am worried this time will be different. Even if I were to be the one to save them, I'd never see them again, and somehow, that seems worse than being made to tend our icy fields.

My mother squeezes my hand, absorbing everything I've laid bare in my gaze and bestowing me a look of love only a mother can give. I swallow down the lump in my throat before pressing a kiss to Sophia's head.

"Forever."

2

———

DOVE

The following morning I find myself tethered to the platform in our town's square.

Freezing wind slashes at my exposed skin. The cold is brutal and the open air platform provides no shelter. My hands and feet have gone numb—I silently curse whoever decided it was customary to await *his* arrival in scraps of fabric.

All I can do is shiver and tuck my legs under myself. Air puffs from between my lips in a frosty cloud. The short chain connecting the iron cuff at my wrist clinks. Glancing down the platform, the five other shaking bodies accompanying me appear to be in the same sorry state. My thin shift sticks to my skin—wet from the flurries floating down on us.

The cloak around my shoulders is the only thing keeping me alive. At least, I think I'm still alive. I can't imagine death being this painful.

Mayor Alrick had said it was the way *the Offering* had always been done: those who were to perform the ritual would arrive barely clothed. If they were chosen, the curse would be lifted, and they would spend eternity draped in the finest silks and softest furs. By the time we had all been chained to the post atop the platform, the cold was burning my lungs, and I stopped listening to much of what he said.

How long would we have to wait up here? When would the townspeople realize the creature wasn't coming and unlock us?

I curse myself for not paying attention to the mayor. Hopefully, by the time we all start turning blue, they'll emerge from the boarded-up tavern across the square and let us go. I'm counting on making it out of this with all my fingers and toes.

Wrapping my arms around my knees, I drop my head down to try and relieve my burning nose. Mama is nearby—locked inside one of the fortified buildings to await the end of the ritual. She had reluctantly brought Sophia along and as much as I don't want her bearing witness to this awful tradition, I find strength in knowing they are both close by.

I can still feel the warmth of their final hugs. Tears had frozen on our cheeks as we parted with promises dining together tonight. Our old, rotting cottage sounds as lovely as a palace. I'd give anything to be warming my toes in front of our crumbling hearth.

Instead, my feet feel the sting of another blustering wind. I have no idea how long we've been up here; it feels like hours. When my mother would come to these in the past, she would be gone all day. At least one family member from each household was required to attend *the Offering*. Papa had done it before his passing, and then the task had fallen to Mama. When I was younger, I was never permitted to attend and then the duty of watching Sophia while Mama was gone became mine.

Now as I sit shackled to this platform, the realization that I know nothing of this process despite now having to participate sinks in.

Mama says she saw him once when she was younger but refuses to talk about it—the sight of him still unsettles her. As I wait tied to this post, hopelessness presses down on me.

Something feels odd—unnerving. Maybe it's just residual anxiety following my run-in with Jon before *the Offering*. He had been waiting near the platform when I arrived. He hadn't even bothered to hide his leer as he openly appraised my body. His presence had put me even more on edge.

Perhaps if I am chosen, that would be another point of comfort. I would save my mother and sister from this harsh weather, and I wouldn't have to marry that awful man. Mama would never force me to, but he wasn't wrong—we could use the money. Watching my mother and sister grow slighter each year would be enough motivation to push me down the aisle.

The wind picks up and flurries of white snow rain down on us. The man next to me groans before doubling over. His fingers and lips are blue. Our eyes connect briefly before his gaze unfocuses. He is familiar to me, but I cannot remember his name. The cold has made it impossible to think.

Snow begins to fall in earnest. It blurs the world around me and quickly obscures the surrounding buildings. My hands tremble as my cloak turns wet. The tips of my ears ache, and more pain lacerates my body.

Maybe we will all die here long before he arrives—if he comes. Wouldn't that just be fitting?

"Have you e—e—ever seen him?" A voice whispers beside me.

The sound nearly gets swallowed up by the wind.

I turn slightly, taking in the girl's blonde hair to my left. Just like with the man, the cold has stolen the memory of her name. The wind burns my face and whips my hair behind me. My shivers have turned violent—my muscles ache with the convulsions.

"No," I say, my voice barely more than a murmur. "Wasn't allowed."

She grits her teeth against the wind.

"I've heard he's f—f—fearsome. A beast with horns and

sharp teeth." Her eyes widen over her pale cheeks. Snowflakes cling to her lashes. "Mrs. Pendleton said the l—l—ast tribute he took was gutted. Right in front of e—every—o—one. The sn—sn—ow never let u—u—p."

I open my mouth to tell her the same thing my mother told Sophia about Pollyanna Pendleton, but my jaw won't work. All of my muscles have frozen. With some panic, I realize I can no longer curl my fingers. The tips of my fingers and toes are turning pale.

For the first time in my life, I welcome death. Anything to end this suffering would be worth it. The faces of my mother and sister appear in my mind, but the burning cold chases them away. There is only shivering—only pain.

I long for it to end—I need it to.

Keeping my eyes open is impossible. The white terrain around me is already a blur. Besides, I have no desire to look death in the face. My body is nothing more than a pile of ice with no chance of thawing in sight. Giving in to the pain, I let go and allow the icy wind to swallow me.

Darkness covers me, and I feel…*warm*. Death's embrace is a raging fire that drags me down into its heated depths. I think of my family—knowing Papa is waiting for me makes this easier. I regret leaving Mama and Sophia, but nothing can save me now.

Something inside my chest clicks—a decision being made, and I'm sucked down deeper in the void. The sound of hooves echoes in my ears as I go under until I hear nothing.

Nothing at all.

3

THE FROST KING

This is a useless task—a yearly ritual he has grown to hate.

It's the only emotion he feels now—hatred. For this task, the snow, and what he did to make things this way. It will be over soon, and he will give himself over to his beast's waiting jaws. Who's to say he hasn't already—it is a rare day the monster isn't in control.

Atop his horse, he can barely see them. He has not been at this settlement in some time. All of these villages look the same, and there are all without what he needs. Even if he can't remember what it is he's been looking far all this time. Still, he must visit them. A different one each year no matter what.

The five figures atop the platform appear as all the others do.

Near death and freezing, their skin blue and their lips cracked. His horse snickers, its head already turning in dismissal. He grabs the reins, ready to return, when something gives him pause.

A biting breeze blows past him, tousling his hair. Its scent causes everything within him to shudder. Turning towards the platform, he wonders how he missed her.

She sits in the center—glowing in comparison to the other humans.

Snowflakes decorate her dark hair. Her round cheeks and full lips are pale. She's fallen onto her side—twitching periodically. It is the only indication she still draws breath.

Something that's laid dormant for centuries rises within him. It pushes to the surface, bringing magic and warmth. It unfurls from his chest and reaches for her.

Her eyelashes flutter on her cheeks and a puff of cold air blooms between her lips. The human's dark eyes lock with his. Gazing into their depths, he nearly falls from his horse. His cold heart hammers against his ribs. A long forgotten feeling tickles the deep recesses of his mind.

The Frost King turns, her scent settling into the marrow of his bones. There is only one word he knows as he stares at her.

Mine.

4

———

DOVE

One moment I'm tumbling through an unending dark, only to find myself thrust into the light.

It's staggering, blazing white, and warm—oh *so* warm. The icy wind that had dug its claws into my flesh has been replaced by a heated, gentle breeze. It's the type of warmth one feels sitting before a roaring fire as it thaws your frozen body. It makes my muscles lose their rigidity. I can flex my fingers and wiggle my toes.

My eyelids flutter. At first I can only make out the thick gloom surrounding me.

It's why I didn't see him at first. Slowly he comes into view. Like a demon from my worst nightmares, he appears through the heavy fog—the *Frost King*.

Only he's not a demon at all. At least not in the way I was envisioning. There are no curling horns and sharp fangs. I'd feel smug about Mrs. Pendleton's status as a liar not being exaggerated if the very real possibility that I was about to die wasn't so present.

His horse blends in with the snow, as does his furlined cape. His face is a smudge of light blue skin that gives way to glittering white hair. It's curly and barely reaches the tips of his arched ears. Nestled atop his head sits a pointed silver crown. Not that he needs it—power radiates from him. Even the snow slows its descent in his presence.

At last, he has come. For a brief moment, I think all of this must be some horrible figment of my imagination. However, the gasps and broken whimpers echoing down the platform, remind me this is all too real.

Did this creature pull me back from the brink of death? For what purpose? My stomach sinks realizing I'm about to find out.

Heavy footsteps stomp along the frozen ground. I remain unmoving atop the platform—the chain around my wrist would prevent me from getting far anyway. Fear grips my heart at his approach. His intense, blue gaze never leaves mine.

Warmth licks over my skin, the same languid touch that pulled me from the darkness. The cold air is no longer painful in my lungs. However, I feel little comfort as he continues his approach. My body screams at me to run—to scream and thrash so that he may be persuaded to choose a more docile tribute.

His eyes never deviate from me, as the world around me fades. Heavy fog encases the Frost King and I on the platform.. I'm transfixed. My heart hammers painfully in my chest. I reach for the fear I felt earlier, arming myself with it before he gets much closer.

Only, the longer I look at him, the less on edge I feel. Magic must be at work here. That is the only way to explain why the tension is leaving my body. My shoulders relax even as my mind screams at me to stay on guard.

The Frost King is not like any human male I have ever seen. With him still mounted on his horse, I can tell he is tall and with thick muscles. High cheekbones taper into his strong, set jaw. Not to mention those eyes. They are brighter than Sophia's, burning with a primal intensity. He is alluring to me in the most unnatural way.

Clearly, I am under his thrall. If he can blight our land he can steal my wits to make me a tame captive.

His horse's nose touches the platform, bringing me within arms reach. A breeze kicks up and blows my hair in front of my eyes. Tucking it away quickly, I watch the Frost King's nostrils flare. Glowing eyes intensify as his blue lips part.

Fresh snow settles on his broad shoulders. Tendrils of my hair cling wetly to my cheeks. A powerful shiver rocks, only this one has nothing to do with being cold. An invisible heated blanket has settled along my shoulders, enveloping me in its warmth. My eyelids droop as drowsiness sets in.

The sound of footsteps echoing down the platform seem far away. A coldness circles my wrist before I hear the manacle crack and fall with a thud next to me. I fight to open my eyes but sleep beckons. I'm too comfortable to fight.

Large hands lift and settle me against a powerful chest.

There is no fear. That is the most damning part of this ordeal. I am going with this creature willingly if only to stay this deliciously warm for as long as possible. Against his chest, another blast of heat settles over me, and I curl towards it. The magic he wields renders me powerless.

I feel his quick intake of breath before one word is growled against my ear.

"*Mine.*"

It clangs around in my head before settling in my heart. I give myself over to this creature and hope that if he does plan to kill me, my mother and sister won't witness it. If I am to die, at least I will go feeling warm and believing that I had some part in breaking this infernal curse.

The Frost King settles me atop his horse. The scent of pine and smoke invades my longs. He tucks me full against him, concealing me from the snow. I burrow further into him as if I can crawl inside the raging inferno roaring in his chest. The reins snap, and the horse below me begins to move.

Cracking my eyes open, I watch heavy snow envelop us. Slumber tempts me with its peaceful darkness. I nearly give in until a scream cuts through the icy fog. A voice—one I'd know anywhere—rises above the wind. It's Mama begging and pleading with all her might. I hear other voices join into the mix. I can picture her fighting and trying to come after me.

The image shocks me into awareness. My eyes fly open, and the warmth surrounding me fades. The icy wind pulls at my wet clothes and hair. I push against the powerful chest and muscular arms caging me.

"L—l—let me g—g—go," I demand through chattering teeth.

My captor glances down at me. I shove against him with all my fading strength. He doesn't even budge.

"L—let m—m—me g—"

Moving faster than I can register, his icy hand wraps around my chin. Forcing my gaze up, his blue eyes blaze into me as if he can peer into my soul.

"Sleep," he commands.

A metallic scent stings my nose as the fight inside me melts away. By the time he drops my chin, my eyelids have shut, and I'm enveloped in a warm, dreamless sleep.

5

THE FROST KING

Something stirs inside his chest as she rests against him. Her breaths curl in puffs of cold air. He can feel her steady heartbeat as warmth returns to her small body. The human's cheeks and lips remain pale and he can't help but wonder what color will they be once she's fully recuperated? Without his magic, she surely would've perished on that wooden beam. The thought of ripping her town to shreds for leaving her in such conditions plays through his mind. His beast would surely like the chance to sink its claws into something.

Soon, that is all he will be.

Looking down at her, her fragility weighs on him as they journey through the mountains. His magic should keep her asleep for most of it.

A long-forgotten emotion nags at him as he watches her eyelashes flutter atop her round cheeks. He has condemned them both—a thought that may have weighed on the mind of the male he used to be. Allowing one final moment to count her breaths, he gives himself over to the creature lurking deep inside him.

A monster that has no concept of remorse.

6

DOVE

The first thing I notice when my eyes open is the mountains.

And how they are on the wrong side of the horizon.

How peculiar. Why would—a blazing cold burns my skin. Icy wind blows against me. The only protection from it is the warmth resting along my back. Letting out a soft moan, I cuddle in deeper, wanting as much of my skin to touch the glorious heat as possible.

Then, in a flash, my memories return. *The Offering*, the cold—the King's thrall on me must have lessened because terror floods my veins. The reality of the situation slams into me with enough force to loosen my muscles.

How long have I been asleep for? Enough time has passed for us to travel over the mountains surrounding my village and end up on the other side. Pulling myself away from his heat is a struggle, but I manage.

The Frost King gives a startled grunt as I push back. His arms cage me to his front. He holds the reins in his large hands while the cold leather of the saddle bites into my legs. I'm tucked tightly between his spread thighs. I need to get off of this and away from him—wherever he's taking me, I'm sure I don't want to go.

Opening my mouth to scream, only a scratchy whisper meets my ears. I shove against his chest, disentangling my legs until they fall on either side of the horse. My toes instantly go numb, but I ignore the pain and focus on my freedom. I have to attempt an escape even if—

"Enough." His voice is powerful—the command shakes snow from the branches around us. "Cease your struggling human, or my magic will put you to sleep once more."

He leads us through a break in the treeline, and we emerge atop a snowy hill. The horse carries us down the mound as I push against him. Thrashing my body, the horse gives an unpleasant whiny but never misses a step. The Frost King keeps one hand on the reins as he moves to grab me. With his arm raised, there's just enough space for me to slip through.

My body falls from the horse and lands with a thud atop a snow pile. The cold shocks me, stealing my breath and instantly soaking me to the bone. My body refuses to move. I was a fool for even trying to escape—where would I go in these clothes? My village could be hundreds of miles away by now.

Death has come to claim me, whether it is at the hands of the snow or the demon with quiet fury raging in his eyes. My surrender comes easy—especially as I watch his massive body jump down from his horse and stomp over to me. The Frost King moves through the snow with unnatural grace. His cloak drags behind him and glimmers in the sun.

The King's strong hands pluck me from the ground and settle my freezing body against him once more. In one fluid motion, we are back on the horse and continuing our journey as if nothing happened. His arm bands across my waist and I feel his lips at my ear.

"Be still," he snarls, causing goosebumps to erupt along my

flesh. "Or I will bind you for the remainder of our journey. You wouldn't enjoy that."

One last burst of anger ignites as I glare at him.

"Let me go." My voice has returned, even if it's a bit scratchy from disuse.

"No."

The simple word turns my burst of anger into a roaring fire. Baring my teeth, I push at his chest even with his arm trapping me. He pulls me flush against him and halts my ability to move. I feel every ridge and contour of his muscular body.

"You were offered to me as a tribute. I claimed you. Your life is mine now to do as I see fit. Remember that."

Air puffs from between my lips.

"Will you be sparing my village from our centuries of torment? Will the blizzard finally let up now that you have taken me?"

The Frost King's eyes narrow before he lets out a humorless laugh.

"Perhaps," he sighs. "If you prove to be a worthy tribute."

Before I can respond, he snaps the reins, and the horse takes off at a swift gallop. The landscape around me blurs. We've left the dense foliage of the evergreen forest. Uphead, the snowy hills give way to a town. The buildings are made of polished white stone and glittering crystals. Everything from homes to taverns and shops dot the hillside. While they are beautiful, something feels off about them.

Namely, there are no people—or whatever manner of creature the Frost King is—milling about. The town is still—lifeless. For a second, I catch something shimmering in the sun, but we are moving too fast for me to make it out properly.

The horse continues at its fast pace, each powerful movement jostling me closer to the Frost King. With my cloak and shift as my only covering, I feel naked in his arms. Something inside my chest flickers, a fleeting feeling of contentment that I push away.

I must remain vigilant. If he has not lifted the curse from my village, then my being taken was for nothing. I will not sacrifice myself without at least trying to better the lives of my family.

The horse slows its pace as we reach a bridge. Made out of the same smooth, white stone the buildings in the town were, it glitters before us. Curving over the fast-moving river below blue water foams and splashes against the rocky sides of the stream. Dense fog lingers on the other side. The sound of clicking hooves echoes as we saunter across it.

The weather here is more mild than in my village. The snow coming down is only a light dusting. With a wave of the King's hand, the fog before us slowly recedes. Once it is cleared the most glorious sight reveals itself.

A palace—the likes of which Mama used to recount to Sophia and me as bedtime stories—made entirely of glass sparkles ahead. The tallest tower reaches into the sky, partially obscured by dense clouds. The windows are decorated with crystal snowflakes and silver. Piles of fresh, white snow decorate the ornately designed ledges. As we journey closer, the sight of the Frost King's castle becomes more imposing.

The horse comes to a stop just before a flight of marble steps. A groan sounds as the two massive glass doors yawn open at our arrival. Behind me, the Frost King slides from the saddle before hooking his hands around my waist and dropping me onto the icy step.

Cold burns my bare feet, and I let out a hiss.

Without his warmth, my wet clothes and hair add to my discomfort. As the wind picks up, I feel my skin prickle. My teeth chatter painfully as shivers wrack me. I tuck my freezing hands under my cloak, which is of little help.

The Frost King stares at me momentarily, surveying me

from head to toe. I try to meet his gaze, but another convulsion rocks me, causing my knees to buckle. With a deep snarl, the Frost King lunges for me. His strong arms go around my back and under my knees. Cradling me to his chest, I don't hesitate to retreat into his warmth.

His steps are clipped as we make our way through the castle. My head fits snugly under his chin, and I fight to keep my eyes open long enough to take in my surroundings. The palace is a labrythin—the further we travel into it, the more confusing it becomes. I lose track of how many steps and turns we take. Countless sets of doors open as we move through dozens of empty rooms. Any chance of remembering the path out is lost after we make what must be our tenth right turn.

Another hallway appears. The dark blue carpet is decorated with what I can only assume is his royal crest—a large silver snowflake, which matches the ones carved on many of the doors. Despite the heat he's putting off, my shivering persists. I try to get closer, but it's not working. My wet clothes feel like they are freezing to my skin, and my trembling intensifies.

The Frost King murmurs something under his breath before making a sharp right—passing us through a stone wall as if it weren't there. The taste of metal lingers on my tongue. He passes us through two more walls before we reach a dark room. The only light comes from a large window against the far wall.

Below it sits a large tub made of dark tiles. Steam curls over the lip. I haven't seen a tub in ages—we sold ours a few years ago for some extra coin. Neither have I ever seen water that warm. Back home, we only heated ours enough to take the chill off. Bathing was a necessity, never a luxury, as I had heard others treat it.

Now, inside this bathroom, I see how someone may wish to spend all day in the bath.

Decadent warmth covers every inch of this room. The

steam coats my skin and helps relieve my shivering. My hands lift to the tie of my cloak and undo the simple knot. The fabric hits the floor with a wet thud. Reaching for the hem of my shift, I can think of nothing but getting this freezing garment off of me.

However, as I try to lift it over my hand, my arms are stiff from the cold. My shivering returns with a vengeance, and soon, my fingers feel too cold even to move. Trembling, I've forgotten I'm not alone until I hear the sound of tearing fabric.

Steamy air greets my exposed back as my shift flutters to the ground to join my soaked cloak. I don't even care that I'm naked. The need to preserve my modesty is not as crucial as the need to feel my fingers and toes again.

With great effort, I move towards the tub, using the final ounces of my strength to heave myself over the side and into the warm water.

I am submerged in glorious heat. Never in my life has anything felt this good. My cold body burns as it thaws in the water. Finally—and only when my lungs scream at me to do so—I surface for air. Pushing my heavy, damp hair out of my eyes, I turn towards the door.

The Frost King is utterly motionless. Unease prickles the back of my neck, even as the flicker in my chest kindles again. Suddenly, I am very aware that I am naked and alone with a creature of unimaginable power. He can walk through walls. He can make me sleep for hours—days even. If he wanted to, he could—

He won't hurt you, a small voice whispers to me. *He can't.*

I must pray to the *Mother of the Snow* that that is true. I wait for him to advance, but he remains still. His fists curl into tight balls at his side. He does not try to glimpse my body, even as I shift in the water and pull my knees to my chest. The Frost King's burning gaze never strays from my face.

His gaze lingers with heat and something else—is an

emotion far too intense for me to name. In an instant, it evaporates, and cool indifference settles over his features.

"Warm yourself," he says simply. "There will be fresh clothes for you in the attached room. That is where you will stay while you are here. I suggest you get familiar with it."

I open my mouth, but he waves a dismissive hand.

"When the bell chimes six times, I expect you to join me for dinner in the main dining hall."

Dinner? A room all to myself? Maybe the stories of the tribute being treated to a life of luxuries weren't too far off. I won't dare allow these basic kindnesses to sway me. I am still his prisoner, and until I find out how I can get him to break the curse on my village, I must always remain vigilant.

Before I can ask where the dining hall is, he disappears in a swirl of white fur leaving behind only a small pile of fresh snow.

7

DOVE

Standing before a large mirror, my hands trail the softest gown I've ever felt.

The light blue satin molds to my body as if it were made just for me. After scrubbing my body and scalp properly, I emerged from the tub, only to be greeted by a warm towel carried by the wind. Invisible hands wrapped it around my wet body while another blotted my hair dry. The taste of metal coated my tongue. The notion of being attended to by the Frost King's magic was a bit jarring.

However, I quickly overcame my shock once I stepped into this lavish room and watched the large wardrobe magically fill with all manner of fine clothes. Thick wool socks hang next to silky stockings and nightgowns. Satin dresses in various shades of blues and whites hang from the racks next to furlined cloaks and scarves.

His magic had helped me dress and even went so far as to conjure a warm breeze to aid in drying my hair. Glossy, loose curls fall to the middle of my back. A portion of it is braided along the crown of my head and secured with a glittering silver pin.

As I continue to study my appearance, color has returned to my face. Behind me, my opulent room is awash in bright sunlight. White light filters in through the massive window across from my large bed, which looks wide enough to sleep ten people. I shared my old bed with Sophia; our feet or arms would have to hang off for us both to fit.

The silky sheets and comforter are soft white, while the mountain of pillows match the dark blue of the bathroom. A massive silver headboard leans against the wall. Besides the bed and the large window, there is a fireplace with a small sitting area and table.

This room is larger than our entire cottage. Guilt creeps in. Here I am in these wonderful clothes, having just had the most glorious bath, and later, I'll sleep in the most incredible bed while my sister and mother wonder if I'm dead.

Tears sting my eyes, but I remind myself that being here is my only chance to save them from the curse. I will do what I must to try and lessen their hardships now that I've been taken captive.

Ice and snow gently hit against the large window. Time must move differently on this side of the mountains. There is no hint of sunset approaching. The sun has remained the same height since we emerged from the trees.

I still don't know how long I've been away. Hours? Days? Weeks? The journey over the mountains could not have been quick. Yet, the Frost King does possess magic. I have to imagine that if he can slide through walls and spell clothes to fit me perfectly, he can travel quickly over the land.

With a deep sigh, I turn from the mirror, only to catch sight of something from the corner of my eye. Pulling back, I look closer at the reflective surface. Inclining my head, I can make out the faintest of shimmering. It rests at the base of my neck under my hair. It is a glittering ball of light. How strange.

Reaching for it, my fingers brush against something warm and soft.

A buzzing sound tickles my ear.

"What the—"

I grab the shimmering orb again but miss it. This is entirely ridiculous. I swat at the thing repeatedly until finally, I raise both my palms, intent on crushing whatever annoying vermin is pestering me.

"STOP!" A shrill voice cuts through the air.

My eyes widen in horror as I watch the orb float in front of my face. It sparkles brilliantly before emitting a soft glow. From its center, a figure emerges. It is distinctly female, curvy, and no larger than my palm. Her blue skin is iridescent, as is her pale blue hair. Gossamer white wings flap at her back. Her eyes glow brightly as she smiles with two dainty rows of razor-sharp teeth.

"Hi," she chirps, giving me a small wave.

My shock at seeing her causes a scream to rip from my lungs. Falling onto my backside, I crawl backwards away from the creature. Frantically, I look for anything to use as a weapon. Kicking off one of my slick slippers, I grip the show in my hand.

Unperturbed by my reaction, the creature flies towards me on her tiny wings. She buzzes before my face—pinching my nose and cheeks with her small hands. I swat at her and push back further, but she merely flies to the side of my head.

"Round," she states, squeezing the top of my ear. "How odd."

I swat her again, but she misses my shoe. Crawling back until my back bumps the far wall, I raise my hands in a defensive potion. The creature just floats in front of me, grinning with her sharp teeth.

"What—what are you?" I ask, failing to keep the tremble from my voice.

"A snow fairy," she replies, primly.

"A snow fairy?"

"Yes, the last one." The glow of her eyes dims. "At least for now."

I eye her warily as she buzzes closer to my face again.

"You've never seen a fairy."

It isn't a question, but I shake my head regardless.

"Well, now you have," she announces proudly, her skin turning a deeper shade of blue.

"Is..." I pause. "Is the Frost King a fairy, too?"

Something flickers in the little creature's gaze before shaking her head.

"An elf." She scrunches her nose. "No wings and cumbersome large bodies. A nightmare if you ask me."

Despite myself, I let out a chuckle. She's made no attempts on my life, so perhaps being afraid of something bigger than a potato is ridiculous. I drop my slipper and slide it back onto my foot. The creature returns my smile and buzzes on happy wings.

"I'm Glimmer," she says. "What's your name?"

I pause for a moment. What's the harm in sharing it? I'm already stuck here.

"Dove."

"Dove," she repeats. "Dove."

Her small hand touches my cheek, a burst of cold against my skin.

"Names are powerful."

I nod, not sure exactly what that means. Rising from the floor, I brush my palms on the skirt of my gown.

"What are you doing here?"

Glimmer shrugs her delicate shoulders before flying over to my bed. She lounges on it with a dramatic flurry of sparkling dust. Rolling onto her stomach, she props her head onto her hands before kicking her feet.

"I was bored. No one's ever in the palace besides the King—seeing a human was quite a surprise."

"Do you know a way out of this place?"

The question is out of my mouth before I can think. It would be good to have an escape route even if I plan to stay until the Frost King lifts the curse on my village. I could have ruined my chances of saving my family if Glimmer decides to report my question to the King.

I expect her to fly off and do so at once, but her color merely dims. Her wings droop at her back, and sad eyes meet mine.

"You can't. No one can, not until—"

The snow fairy breaks off in a fit of coughs. Her body shakes as she hacks through it. She shakes her head before muttering something about tricky magic. Her wings flap, and she flies towards me. I don't know what motivates me, but I lift my hand, and her cool body fits snugly in my palm.

"I forgot how little I'm able to say." At my confused expression, she goes on. "If you want to leave this place, you must listen to the King. He's the only one who can save you."

"Save me? He's the one who brought me here—the one who cursed my village."

Glimmer shakes her head.

"Nothing is what it seems here."

I let out a huff.

"You aren't making sense."

The snow fairy's wings sag once more.

"That's what she intended."

"Who?" I ask.

"The sorceress, the one who—"

Again, Glimmer breaks off in a fit of coughing. Using my finger, I gently rub circles on her back until it subsides. Glimmer smiles up at me.

"My tongue can be loosened more so than the King's, but I am still not immune to what has been done."

I nod, trying to sift through the riddles and half-truths that are all of her sentences.

"I just want to get back to my family." Sadness washes over me.

Glimmer's eyes lower, and her lips part, but before she can speak, six loud chimes of the tower bell echo around us. Unease turns my stomach, realizing that my evening is far from over.

The snow fairy flutters to my pointer finger and grips it with both hands.

"Come. I'll lead you to the dining hall. The King has never been a very patient male." At my lowered brows, Glimmer's cheeks blaze dark blue. "I may have been eavesdropping, but only a little."

Despite myself, my lips tug upwards as the fairy pulls me from the room. We travel down the hallway in silence. The dark blue carpet drags beneath my slipper-clad feet. The walls are lined with windows showing off the light snowfall and the sparkling buildings below. Silver motifs and designs adorn the marble walls as we walk.

It's eerily quiet. Only the sound of my breathing and Glimmer's flapping wings can be heard. Our path is just as confusing as the one the Frost King led me on. We pass by great halls and sparkling ballrooms adorned with crystal chandeliers.

Despite the grandeur, the castle has a distinct look of disarray. Frost licks over exposed cracks in the wall. Most of the furniture is covered with sheets or removed from the walls, leaving behind old nails and some wires.

We keep traveling deeper within the castle until Glimmer stops me outside two massive double doors. Like all the others, a large snowflake has been carved and backfilled with silver on each one. Glimmer drops my finger and flies up in front of my face.

Her glowing eyes are serious.

"There isn't much time," she whispers. "Your freedom—all of our freedom—hinges on the King."

I lick over my dry lips.

"And he can't just let me go. What happens if I try to leave?"

Glimmer shakes her head. "The magic would stop you."

I roll my eyes. "Great. Well then, I better get started on figuring out...whatever it is you want me to figure out."

The snow fairy nods, deepening her color.

"Nothing is what it seems."

"You mentioned that already."

Glimmer purses her lips before buzzing up to my ear. I feel her soft hands hold onto my hair.

"Find the secrets hidden within the past. If you do, all this shall pass."

I pull back silently and arch a brow.

"Did you just rhyme past with pass?"

Glimmer gives me a grin before beginning to shimmer. In a moment, she is nothing more than a whisper of sparkling, blue fairy dust. With a deep sigh, I turn back towards the door. I have no idea what will await me on the other side.

All I can hope for is figuring out what's happening before it's too late.

8

———

THE FROST KING

She sits stiffly at the end of the table.

She does not speak a word. He watches her through the eyes of the beast. Her color has returned—the bath has restored her glow and brought a shine to her hair. The dress molds to her body, the same one he had glimpsed when—

He swallows down a snarl, refusing to give the memory any purchase in his head.

They have not spoken a word to each other. From the moment she arrived in the dining hall, looking like a vision from his sweetest dreams, tense silence surrounded them. However, the beast does not dream or understand the need for this farce. It is a pointless waste of time.

He should be preparing, not having a tense dinner with someone he never should've taken.

"Fool," a voice snarls from deep inside him. "Let me out before you ruin everything."

This voice is familiar—it makes his hackles lower.

"You remember me," it says. "Remember who you are. It is not too late. There is still time."

The beast feels warm. Warm enough to let the exhaustion of keeping up his icy walls dissipate. He doesn't have it in him to fight right now. Not when the sweet release of a nap beckons him into the darkness.

Yes, he will rest now and make preparations later.

"Very good old friend," the voice praises.

He lets the familiar voice wash over him, feeling something knitting back together and becoming whole.

Friend, the voice had called him. It's odd. The beast cannot remember ever having one of those.

9

DOVE

Setting my fork next to my empty plate, I dare a glance at my silent dinner companion.

While the food had been delicious—no doubt magically prepared—it was nothing compared to Mama's cooking. It lacked her most important ingredient: love. The food quality had been better than any I'd ever had—my steak was tender enough to cut with a fork—and yet I would gladly never taste it again to be sitting at my mother's table once more. Both of us chatting happily while Sophia recounted some tale she thought up throughout the day.

Instead, I sit in a high-back chair with my stomach in knots. The Frost King seems more surly than this morning. He barely acknowledged my presence before ushering me to sit on the opposite side of the table. No pleasantries were exchanged. I merely picked up my fork and started eating.

My growling stomach had motivated me to eat without considering it could be poison. However, from what Glimmer said, I'm essential in uncovering what is happening here. I glance down at the knife next to my plate. It probably would've been wise to search for a weapon. This dull blade would do minor damage against someone as powerful as the Frost King.

From my brief glance, I saw him staring at nothing. He hadn't eaten anything, merely sipped from a goblet of wine and looked through me. It was unsettling, to say the least.

Suddenly, he jerks sharply. Unease prickles my neck as his eyes close. He shivers in his chair, thrashing slightly before he exhales.

His eyes pop open, and they are different—in fact, all of him seems changed.

His skin glows bright blue, and his eyes look less animalistic. He is almost human, especially in how he stares at me. Inhaling deeply, his nostrils flare. His mouth and muscles lose all their tension.

His eyes spark with recognition as a soft, apologetic smile curls his lips, and he ducks his head. I rear back in my chair, unsure what to make of this sudden transformation.

"I fear I have been unfair to you," he states.

Even his voice is different—deep but softer, not as gravely. I blink at him, the only indication I've heard what he said. Despite my silence, he presses on.

"I...apologize for my behavior. That is not how I wanted your first impression of me to be." He shakes his head, silver crown sparkling in the light. "You must be confused—scared. I mean you no harm, truly."

Arching a brow, I can't help my laugh of shock.

"You expect me to believe that?"

The Frost King cringes at my sharp tone.

"I know it's hard to believe. I've given you no reason to trust my word, but I promise it's true. I won't hurt you."

I remain silent as his gaze lingers on mine.

"Your purpose here cannot be overstated."

I laugh once more, rolling my eyes.

"Is that what you tell all the tributes you've stolen?"

I'm surprised at my boldness. I should be falling to his feet and pleading for mercy, but I find myself needing to nettle him —to make him understand that I am no helpless captive. The minute my freedom is within my grasp, I will take it. Whether I figure out the mysteries afoot here or not.

The King looks away from me.

"I've never taken on before."

My mouth falls open at his confession. What does this mean for me? Why have I been chosen?

"Before you ask me why I haven't, don't bother. I cannot say. Not yet, at least."

Turning back towards me, he takes a sip of wine before exhaling another breath.

"There are forces at work here—ones beyond my control."

"How is that possible?" I ask. "You are the Frost King—you rule over all. You caused the blight on our land."

His chuckle lacks all warmth.

"Whoever made you believe that is a fool. In time, you will learn just how little power I have."

Anger rises within me.

"I don't have time for all this—I need to return to my family," I snap.

His eyes flare, but his mouth remains closed. Anger has not aided me in gaining my freedom. It could be wise to try a different approach. Reluctantly, I gentle my tone.

"Please," I say. "Let me go. My mother and sister—they won't survive without me."

Again, another heated emotion flashes in his gaze. His jaw tightens.

"Please," I say again, moisture stinging my eyes. I will myself not cry. Tears solve nothing.

"Your family has been taken care of."

Ice floods my veins, and my stomach turns.

"What does that mean?"

Instead of answering, the Frost King raises his hand. I gasp as ice swirls around his open palm. A fresh pile of snow glimmers as he shapes it into a perfectly round ball. The scent of metal dances in the air as he rolls the snowball towards me. It leaves behind a wet trail on the table.

"See for yourself." He nods towards the tightly packed snow.

Lifting it, I feel the snow hum with power. Cold kisses the tips of my fingers as I examine it. The ball's surface swirls into a hazy blue mist. My heart pounds in my chest. It takes a moment for it to focus, and then fresh tears spring to my eyes when it does.

It is our cottage. Only it has been significantly repaired. The wood flooring and walls are new. The kitchen table glitters from the light of a roaring fire. Atop it is stacked all manner of food and desserts. Mama is in her usual spot, wearing a new green wool gown. Sophia is also in a new dress—the dark brown fabric matches her hair. There is a place set for me even as no food is ladled onto it. Both Mama and Sophia share a smile, even if their eyes are sad. At least they aren't starving— far from it.

In an instant, the vision is lost, and the white surface of the snowball remains still.

"My magic will keep them safe." The King's low voice reaches me. "They won't go hungry as long as you're here. You have my word."

I eye him warily as the snowball begins to melt through my fingers. It falls to the table with a wet slap.

"How can I trust you're telling the truth? How can I believe what I saw was real and not some foul trick of your magic?"

The King's blue eyes narrow slightly before shaking his head.

"I cannot lie to you. It's one of my many punishments."

"Punishment for what?"

The Frost King waves a dismissive hand.

"I'm dangerously close to saying too much already."

Rising from his chair, it scrapes against the tile floor. My heartbeat picks up as he rounds the table. He has removed his cape from earlier. He wears simple wool pants and a linen shirt with silver threading—his crown sparkles atop his head. The open collar of his shirt peels back, and I glimpse the hard contours of his chest. The memory of those muscles pressing against me floods my mind and heat spreads up my neck.

I want to kick myself for such a reaction. The Frost King is why I'm trapped here—thinking about his muscles is not bringing me any closer to freedom.

He continues to prowl towards me, his eyes glowing with awareness.

"My magic won't keep him away for long. Soon, there won't be enough to keep him contained at all."

The King reaches me, and before I can ask what he's doing or who he's referring to, he drops to his knees at my side. I stop breathing as he reaches a tentative hand out. He skims a finger over each of my cheeks. I should be recoiling—slapping his hand away and demanding he never touch me again. What I shouldn't be doing is reveling in the sensation of his touch. As his finger skims over my cheek again, I am barely able to swallow down my moan.

I've never been touched like this by a male—elf or human. This has to be some trick, but the metallic scent of magic is missing. After a long day of traveling, the exhaustion must finally be catching up with me.

Obviously, I'm delirious from the journey and have lost my wits.

The Frost King inhales deeply, holding his breath as if savoring my scent. His eyes fall closed as his hand fully cups my cheek. The weight of it is terrifying and pleasant at the same time.

"You are my only hope," he whispers. "I truly am sorry for bringing you into all of this. My actions were selfish—the same selfishness that got me into this mess in the first place. But when I saw you, I knew."

"Knew what?" My cheeks heat at the breathy sound of my voice.

He shakes his head, white tendrils flopping over his pointed ears.

"It's not time to share all of that." His eyes open, and they pin me to my chair with their heated stare. "Not because I don't want to but because I can't. The more you learn, the easier it is for us to speak. That is the nature of that damned sorceress's c—"

He breaks off in a fit of coughs. It is as if the words were pulled from his mouth and the air sucked from his lungs. He coughs once more, his eyes outlined in red.

"Please," he begs. The longing in his gaze burns me alive. "You can save us—save me. It's always been you."

A grimace mares his full lips, and the veins in his neck protrude.

"He's waking up now," The King groans. "Remember, the truth is buried deep. When the moon is high, the three stars will guide you to the key."

His words are utter nonsense.

"I don't understand. None of you speak plainly."

Blue lips pull into a painful grin. His fingers on my face tighten as if he cannot bear to let me go.

"I've been waiting for you—longing all these centuries."

A loud groan rips from his mouth as he doubles over on his knees. I watch in horror as the blue tinge to his skin loses its luster. His eyes turn feral and his mouth pulls into a sneer. The hand on my cheek is ice cold before he violently rips it away with a snarl.

His eyes are two blocks of ice chasing away any warmth I felt.

"Go to your room and stay there," he commands, his voice returning to how it was this morning. "This dinner is over."

His eyes rove over me with thinly veiled contempt. I've had just about enough of all of this. Between Glimmer's riddles and the King's duel personalities, my head is starting to throb. I push back in my chair with force.

"What is going on? You can't say—"

The Frost King raises his hand, now tipped with deadly sharp claws. I swallow my words, my mouth running dry. The scent of metal invades my lungs.

"Enough," he says bitterly.

With a wave of his hand, I'm thrown from the room. Invisible hands pull me through walls, my body passing through each one effortlessly. The magic encases my skin, making it feel oily. Twisting and turning through hallways and rooms, my stomach tips. My dinner races up my throat as the castle swirls around me.

I'm slammed into my body as my feet land inside my room. The door is open, and I rush towards it only for a strong wind to slam it shut in my face. Trying the handle is of no use. I'm locked inside.

Pounding my fist against the heavy stone door, I scream all my frustrations out against it.

"Let me out! Let me out!"

Tears burn in my eyes and pour down my cheeks. My hands ache from banging against the unforgiving surface. Everything I've shoved down rises to the surface, and I let it overflow. I cry and cry and cry until there is nothing left. Sliding to the floor, I tuck my knees against my chest and allow the sobs to subside.

This is the most confused I've ever been.

How can I uncover whatever plot is afoot here when no one makes any sense? The King looks at me with such longing that it tempts me to consider things I've never done before, only to turn into a beast that tosses me from the room without a second thought. How am I supposed to navigate such a male?

Glimmer and the King have both alluded to secrets buried deep. Whatever that means. If I can get back to my family by uncovering whatever this sorceress did here, I must try.

Even if I have no clue where to begin.

10

THE FROST KING

It was foolish to let the other part of him out.

Almost as foolish as the dinner. He knows the end is coming, and nothing can prevent it. The cold in his body is growing more intense—settling into the marrow of his bones and turning his blood to ice. Soon, there will be nothing left, not even the beast.

Bringing her here was a mistake. He never should've given in to the weak male inside of him.

Indeed, she will turn from him now. Why did he even want her in the first place?

The beast does not know, nor does he care.

At least, that's what he tells himself as he stands outside her door. She is not asleep. He can hear her uneven breaths and the sound of her rustling sheets. The thought of going into her room is fleeting. One that is not unpleasant but all the same unwelcome.

Her rejection will come swiftly, leaving him to his dreadful future—the one of his own making.

Inhaling her lovely scent one last time, he turns from her door and vows never to find himself outside of it again.

11

DOVE

Sleep eludes me after that tumultuous dinner.

I still feel on edge after my confusing exchanges with the King. More than that, the sun never seems to set here. As I lay tucked under ridiculously soft sheets with dozens of cloudlike pillows resting behind me, bright light streams under the heavy curtains covering the window.

All concepts of time are lost in this place. If I am not careful and remain dedicated to my desire to escape, I may lose myself to the strangeness of this land.

My only small comfort this evening is the King's promise to keep my family safe. While I have no reason to trust him, I believe he was telling the truth. He seems to need me for whatever reason, and with my family safe, I'm more amenable to his cause than an escape attempt.

At least for the time being.

His words were not lost on me—my family is safe for now as long as I remain here and try to undo whatever foul magic is afoot. *I cannot lie to you, it is one of my many punishments*, he had said, but what was he being punished for? If I can uncover the reason, perhaps I'll be one step closer to getting out of here.

That may be easier said than done, seeing as no one here can give a straight answer to save their life. Whatever spell this sorceress cast upon all of them is binding. Annoyingly so. My head continues to throb.

With a deep sigh, I rise from the bed, hissing as my feet touch the icy floor. I quickly shove them into warm, fur-lined slippers. I find a heavy wool robe inside the wardrobe and belt it over my silk nightgown. The room is bright enough that I don't need candlelight to guide me.

Gently closing the doors to the wardrobe, I make my way over to the far wall. The curtains had been drawn when I arrived as the same magical force from before prepared me for bed. Now, I grip the heavy fabric and wrench it back in my hands.

Staggering light pours into the room. The snow-packed evergreen trees and small buildings dotting the edge of the palace grounds shimmer below. Only it's not sunlight causing them to glow. Where the large orb of white light had once sat nestled between wispy clouds has been replaced by a large blue moon. With the curtains no longer obscuring it, the light inside my room takes on a blue-ish hue.

It is magnificent. Usually, the clouds in my village are too thick to see the moon, let alone the stars. Here, both are on full display. Countless stars twinkle down from their resting spots in the dark sky. It's easy to forget where I am for a moment—to allow myself to absorb the sky's simple beauty.

Taking a few steps back from the window to enjoy the view better, I'm struck again by how still everything seems here. There is no movement, no hum of life. In my village, even as remote as our cottage was, there were signs of life all around me. Neither Mama, Sophia, nor I could sit still for long, and there was always work to be done. Our town was the same whenever we would venture into it. People hustling from one job to the next or those with extra coin could enjoy a hot meal and mug of mulled wine at the tavern.

On this side of the mountain, there is none of that. There is no indication that anyone besides myself draws breath here. For the first time, I feel totally and utterly alone. No amount of fine clothes, food, or bedding can make up this feeling of complete isolation.

My heart pangs, and even though I owe him nothing, and he is the one who brought me to this desolate place, I can't help but feel bad for the King. Being left to live in a place like this, it's no mystery how he's acquired his peculiar personality.

Despite believing him to be the one who cursed us, my village knows very little of the Frost King. Stories have been changed throughout generations. Once, he had been a disgraced farmer who made a deal with the *Mother of the Snow* for untold riches and, in his greed, cursed the land to attain it. In others, he was a beast, roaming the snowy peaks of the mountain, cursing our village on a whim for not offering him enough meat to feast on.

The heart of each of the stories remains the same. The Frost King can control the weather, and due to some slight by a member of our village, he doomed our land to endure an eternal winter, each year becoming more brutal than the last. Annually, he comes to select a tribute, and if one is chosen, he will release the land from his magic.

While I've never heard of anyone leaving our village, the few travelers who pass through all share similar stories. They suffer under the same wintery conditions and offer up their own human tributes to please him. All of us are forced to live under his thumb. The cold weather keeps us all hungry and weak enough to never fight back—the conditions for travel are treacherous at best. Even if someone wanted to mount an offensive against him, they could never make the journey here.

He was the cause of all my hardships—the one I pictured when the harvests were low, and Sophia and I shivered in our bed as cold air ripped through our cottage. However, as I stare out the large window to the still land below, I can't help but feel like the blame was misplaced.

The King is just as much a prisoner as I am.

That is a dangerous thought—I try to shove it away as I look again towards the sky. Three stars glow brighter than the others. One resides below in the center, while the other two are slightly higher and flank both sides. The moon rests above the odd formation.

I take a few steps back until the window frames it. The stars with the moon resting above make the perfect arrowhead shape, pointing to the ground below. Three stars. Hadn't the King mentioned something about three stars?

When the moon is high, the three stars will guide you to the key.

Taking another tentative step back, I gasp as the stars perfectly line up with the stones framing the window. They are pale in color and have the same smooth texture from which the palace walls are made. The one resting under the star in the middle is different, however. It glows with a gentle blue hue, shimmering in the moonlight, while the others remain matte and pale.

Surely not, I think.

Reaching toward the glittering stone, its smooth surface is warm as it greets my palm. Pulsing with life, it hums in my grip. I give it a sharp tug, but nothing happens. Its color dims as if annoyed by my efforts. I try again, to no avail.

With a huff, I shove my fingers in as deep as they will go until they bump into the wall it's nestled into. There is enough of a gap that if—

Twisting my wrist sharply, a light pop sounds and the stone drops into my palm.

I don't get to thoroughly inspect the rock until a loud, groaning sound rattles behind me. Whipping towards it, I watch as the wall next to my bed shudders until a small door splits from the wall and peels open. Frost and dust fall to the floor as a strong wind blows in from the newly revealed dark corridor.

There has been no groove in the wall indicating anything was there. *The truth is buried deep*—maybe I'll find some of it through there. The stone pulses in my hand, glowing brighter with encouragement. As if my time here couldn't get any stranger, I'm allowing a stone to guide me through a hidden passageway. My common sense shakes its head, but logic and reason are far from this palace.

Passing through the door, I see that this corridor has been abandoned for some time. Old wooden beams line the ceiling —cracked and dusted with crystalized spider webs. The walls are made of simple gray stones, as is the floor. The stone in my palm lights the way as a gentle breeze blows through me. The temperature is mild, and the scent of pine dances through the air.

The sound of my breathing feels out of place in the quiet hall.

After walking for what feels like hours, the stone flares in my palm as we reach the end of the corridor. My feet halt on the other side of a wooden door with chipped blue paint. The design on the golden handle has worn down in places from use. The stone pulses, warming the skin of my hand until it burns. That's all the signal I need to reach for the handle and twist it open.

The room is barren, save for one polished wood table at the center. As I walk towards it, I see an engraving of the Frost Mountains etched into the surface. Whoever did it had remarkable skill, and the textures seem life-like. Along the edges of the table are the drawings of snow fairies. Some are in flight on their tiny wings, while others are resting on evergreen branches. Each one is depicted with a mischievous smile.

At the center of the table rests a small blue velvet pillow. Atop it sits a necklace. The pendant, made of gleaming white stone, is shaped like a snowflake and hung on a delicate silver chain. I'm transfixed by it. It's the most beautiful piece of jewelry I've ever seen.

"*Take it,*" a voice whispers. "*Take it and see what has been forgotten.*"

Swallowing soundly, I reach for the necklace.

"And now I'm listening to a disembodied voice," I mumble. "What's the worst that can happen?"

My fingers brush over the smooth surface of the snowflake. It is not stone but a large crystal, iridescent in the low light.

The scent of metal burns my lungs. Similar to how I felt when the King sent me flying back to my room earlier, the world around me shifts and tilts. It is as if I'm inside my body, but I am also a spectator watching as I am thrown through time. Shifting and rolling, the world around me is a mass of darkness and glittering dust.

Then everything stops, and I land on my feet inside a room.

I blink to adjust my vision. The room looks familiar. Glancing down, I see the table I had just been standing at, with its etchings of mountains and snow fairies. Only this time, the room is not barren, and I am not alone.

Tiny, decorative furniture covers the marble floor. From a small bed with blue sheets and pillows to a low workbench decorated with crude drawings and piled high with small books. A fireplace snaps and roars off to the side. A chest engraved with some markings is seated in the corner. Pictures of the castle and a few portraits of a baby wrapped in a silver blanket line the walls.

Everything in the room is fuzzy, blurry at the edges, as if I am in a dream.

No, it's not a dream, I think, *but a memory.*

It is not one of my own. That becomes clearer when I register the two figures sitting together on a high-back chair in the corner of the room.

The older male looks up and directly through me, solidifying that I am not here but merely witnessing what once was. The male has fine wrinkles dotting his pale blue-colored face. His white hair is long, nearly brushing his chest. There is a proud set to his posture. His clothes are sturdy and adorned with metals that sparkle. As does the silver crown atop his head, the same one the King wears.

Glancing down at the small child in his lap, the breath freezes in my lungs as I take in the young male's sparkling blue eyes. The ones I saw at dinner. The King does not seem so scary as a small child. He was pretty adorable with his round cheeks, small pointy ears, and thick white curls. He's dressed in a simple pair of blue silk pants and a matching shirt.

The older male holds him on his knee, the snowflake pendant dangling before the young male's dazzling eyes. The father looks at him warmly, but there's a sadness swimming in his gaze.

"It was your mother's," the older male says softly. He hands it to the boy, letting it dangle from his tiny hand. "One day, it will be yours to bestow upon another."

The young boy furrows his white brows. "But how will I know who to give it to?"

Blue lips pull into a grin before kissing the side of the young male's head.

"You'll know, my son," he says gently. "The snowflake will guide you home. Even if all seems lost."

The little elf's eyes look away from the necklace and connect with mine. He gives a small gasp as something flashes in his gaze.

The memory around me disappears instantly as if I have

been plucked from a bath. Once more, I am back inside this barren room, my fingers still resting atop the necklace. The snowflake glows brightly and warms my fingers. Gently, I lift it from the pillow and hold it before myself. Is this the key the King had been referring to? Let's hope so.

Even with that glimpse of his memory, I'm still at a loss for what happened here, nor do I know what I am supposed to do to solve what's afflicting the land. Will returning this necklace be the answer? I can only pray the solution is that simple. I tuck the necklace into my robe pocket and lift the glowing stone in my hand again.

The wooden table creaks and snaps before disintegrating into a pile of dust carried away on a breeze. As the room begins to tear itself apart, I quickly make my way back out through the door and into the corridor. The blue paint on the door flakes off further until the wood splinters before melting into the gray stones of the wall.

As if nothing had ever been there.

Making my way back up the corridor, the memory I had just witnessed leaves me reeling. Something about it nags at me, begging me to look deeper, but I don't know how. What was I supposed to uncover from that interaction between the King as a child and his father? Is his father somehow responsible for what happened here? I saw nothing but love between the two, even if the older male was still mourning the mother of his child.

The pounding in my head comes back with a vengeance as I, at last, make it back to my room. Returning to the window, I push the stone back into place with a click. The door at the wall rumbles before swinging shut and blending into the wall—no trace of the opening to be found.

I kick off my slippers and crawl into bed.

We've never heard stories of another Frost King. That memory must've been from some time ago. Its significance cannot elude me forever, but for now, sleep beckons. As I turn on my side, I feel the snowflake necklace in my pocket resting along my hip and pulsing with power.

It pins me to the bed as if it carries the weight of a million secrets.

12

DOVE

Tiny hands pinch my cheeks and tickle my nose.

I half-heartedly swat at them. It's too early. Even with my eyelids closed, I can tell bright sunlight is streaming into my room. Another pinch is delivered to my nose, and I swipe a hand at the one pestering me.

"Watch it!" Glimmer's squeaky voice snarls in my ear.

"Go away," I mumble. Burrowing into a pillow, I try to ignore her ever-present buzzing. "I'm sleeping."

I don't have to see Glimmer to know she's turned a deep shade of blue.

"Get up," she declares. "Your breakfast is getting cold."

My grumbling stomach rouses me, and I peek one eye open. With a sigh, I crawl out from my warm swath of blankets. The sunlight is blazing. Not pulling back the curtains after last night's adventure was a mistake. My eyes adjust slowly until a small, sparkling figure comes into view.

Glimmer grins at me, her tiny teeth looking extra sharp this morning.

"Morning," she chirps.

"Morning," I say, stretching my arms above my head.

Despite having slept on the most luxurious mattress, my muscles feel sore. All that magic traveling over mountains, through walls, and *now* into the past clearly takes a toll on the human body. Kicking my feet over the side of the bed, I shove them in my slippers and follow Glimmer's gossamer wings over to the sitting area before the fireplace.

The snapping flames send licks of heat over my body. Glancing down at the silver tray, it is laden with all manner of breakfast items. There are eggs—a delicacy back in my village—salt-cured pork, thick slices of pale-colored cheese, steaming rolls, and two different types of jam.

It looks perfect except for the tiny teeth marks marring the meat and rolls. I raise a brow at Glimmer.

"Helped yourself, did you?"

The snow fairy's cheeks go up in blue flames.

"Just making sure it wasn't poisoned," she delicately corrects. "That's all."

"Mm-hm."

Settling into the nearest chair, I slice off a good portion of the meat she'd been nibbling on and hand it to her. Her eyes glow brightly as she clasps the greasy pork between her tiny hands—gnawing and suckling with her sharp teeth. I can't help but laugh at the sight. Taking my own bite of the meat, the salty flavor causes me to groan.

Having finished the pork and most of the eggs, I'm buttering a roll when Glimmer buzzes excitedly in front of my face.

"How was dinner with the King?"

Licking over my teeth, I take a bite instead of answering. Glimmer settles beside me on the armrest as she awaits my response.

"He is an interesting male," I say, swallowing. "The King has your fondness for speaking in riddles."

Glimmer nods sadly. "That's one of the unfortunate parts of the c—c—cu—c—."

"Curse?" I offer.

The snow fairy glows brightly, moving swiftly to hover before me.

"Did the King tell you about it?" Her excitement is palpable.

I give a slight shrug. "Not in so many words. I pieced it together during our dinner."

Polishing off the last of my roll, I level a stare at the snow fairy.

"What do you know about the sorceress behind all of this?"

Glimmer's color dims to a sickly pale blue.

"We shouldn't speak of her. She'll return soon if you can't break it in time."

"And you don't have any idea how I could possibly do that?"

Sadness tips the tiny fairy's lips. "No. I wasn't even here when the curse was cast."

At my lowered brows, Glimmer settles atop my turned-over teacup.

"I was away—deep in the forest, avoiding my responsibilities. I never could've imagined what I would return to." Her color dims further as her wings sag. "Life was different back then. Hundreds of us snow fairies lived in our fortress in the woods. From what I remember, the frost elves and my people got along. It's blurry now, as are the years before the curse. All I know is that the King was being punished for something, and we all had to suffer for it. The details of how and why are missing."

Shimmering eyes stare up at me.

"By the time I returned and learned what had been done, this land had become barren, and my people—"

Her body jerks as she breaks off into a sob. My heart aches for this tiny creature all alone in this world. What kind of sorceress punishes all for the faults of one? A better question might be, what kind of male is the King to have incurred such a wrath?

Until I better understand who he is and what he's done, I can't determine whether this punishment is just. Right now, I think it's a bit overkill.

Reaching down, I cup Glimmer in my palm. Her curvy body settles there as I soothe her with gentle strokes down her back. Wiping away at her eyes, her smile is sad.

"It was dark magic she used. Our bodies are so small—they froze in an instant. I would've joined the rest of my kind in time, but since I was away when the curse was struck, I was spared from the initial wave. I live under the same conditions the King must adhere to. He doesn't have much longer. Everywhere the curse touches will get worse very soon." She grips my thumb, rubbing her face against it. "I cannot even remember what my family looks like or their names. Every passing day, the curse takes more of my memories, and I fear the day there will be none left."

Moisture stings my eyes.

"I'm so sorry, Glimmer."

The snow fairy nods before giving me a triumphant smile.

"But you're gonna save us, right?"

Sadness encases my heart in ice, but I return her grin.

"I'm going to try," I say, leaning back in my chair.

The movement causes something heavy to hit my outer thigh. Everything from last night comes rushing back.

"The King gave me a riddle last night at dinner," I explain. "It didn't make much sense then, but I figured it out and discovered a hidden passageway where I found this."

Digging into my pocket, I pull out the snowflake necklace. In the sunlight, its cloudy white crystal sparkles and refracts the light. A thousand incandescent colors dance on its surface. Glimmer gasps, touching a pointed tip of it with her hand.

"Have you ever seen this?"

"Yes," she breathes. "Around the throat of a queen."

A queen. The Frost King's mother. Is she connected to all of this somehow?

"It's more than just a necklace. Its magic is powerful—elemental. How did you find it?"

I cringe. "A glowing rock led me to it."

Glimmer nods as if that is the most normal answer in the world.

"It wanted you to find it for a reason. Perhaps it will lead you to—"

A knock sounds at my door.

Glimmer flies from my hand in a flash of sparkling wings and nestles herself on my shoulder. Quickly tucking the snowflake necklace back into my pocket, I rise from the chair.

"Who is it?" I call and quickly slap a hand to my forehead.

No one else lives here. What kind of question is that?

"It's me," the King responds. "Can I come in?"

His voice is gentle with a hint of amusement. My face flushes, but I am at least pleased that it is this version of him outside my door and not the one that so casually locked me in here last night.

"Yes."

The lock on the door clicks before gently swinging open on silent hinges. The King is there, looking much like he did last night in his simple pants and silver-trimmed shirt. His crown still neatly rests atop his snow-white head. His eyes glow differently as he appraises me from head to toe. My stomach dips at his attention, and I feel naked even with my thick robe covering me.

A gentle smile plays on his lips as he walks closer. My heart hammers painfully in my chest. Light flares along my side, the necklace in my pocket blazing unrestrained. The King's eyes dip towards it.

Having no choice but to reveal it, I pull the jewelry from my pocket and extend it towards him. The King's eyes widen as he slowly extends a finger to trace along the pendant before taking it into his large hands. His scent of pine and spice invades my nostrils.

"You found it," he says. "Clever girl."

His praise sets my cheeks on fire.

"It belonged to my mother," he says, confirming my earlier suspicion. "I'd forgotten all about it. It's been centuries since I last saw it. I—I don't know why."

He swallows audibly before his gaze slams into mine. Gratitude dances in his fiery blue eyes. I could drown in their intensity. Our chests nearly brush as I take a deep breath. He tempts something dangerous inside of me—it urges me to forget why I'm here, even if it would be unwise to do so.

Clearing my throat, I give him a brief nod.

"I'm glad I could return it to you."

The King's eyes linger on my face. I feel his stare as if it was a physical touch. A soft chuckle passes through his full lips. Shaking his head, he takes a step closer towards me.

"My father gave it to me to bestow as I see fit. I want you to have it."

I blink at him, my mouth falling open.

"Me? No, I couldn't possibly—"

"Please. Allow this to be my first gesture towards apologizing for my abhorrent behavior last night."

Licking over my dry lips, I nod, not trusting my voice. He smiles, and my insides turn warm. Heat pours off of him and teases my skin. What magic is he using on me to feel this way? It threatens to thaw away my icy resolve.

Walking around me, I feel him move my hair over my shoulder. His fingertips skim down the back of my neck, and I can't stop the sigh that leaves my lips. His touch kindles something dangerous in me. I've never craved the touch of another like this. I used to dream about the embrace of a man, but only in the abstract. Now, with the King's fingers teasing my skin, this brief touch is more wonderful than I ever imagined.

The pendant rests in the hollow of my throat. The crystal is cool against my warm skin. As he secures the clasp, he gently moves my hair back. Instantly, I miss his touch. What is happening to me?

"I see you've met the smallest nuisance our castle has to offer," he laughs, standing before me once more.

A furious buzzing sound echoes by my ears, and my face flames anew. *Glimmer.* I had completely forgotten all about her nestled under my hair. With a dramatic twirl, the snow fairy turns dark blue before crossing her arms over her chest and pouting at the King.

"A nuisance? How rude. Dove and I are friends."

The King's eyes return to me, his mouth parting slightly.

"Dove," he sighs, as if tasting the word. I try not to shiver at the utter delight swimming in his gaze. "That is your name?"

I nod, realizing that he never asked me for it. Nor have I asked for his.

"It's beautiful," he whispers. "Almost as beautiful as you."

Before I can respond, Glimmer flutters between us, breaking the King's stare.

"Old Frosty must've lost all his manners if he hasn't even bothered to learn your name."

With one last huff, Glimmer disappears into a cloud of sparkling dust. The King shakes his head, peering down at me. With his height, I must lean back to meet his gaze. His compliment still rings in my ears. What should I even say to something like that?

Ignoring it is my best bet, and I do just that.

"Frosty? Is that your name?"

The Frost King chuckles before shrugging.

"It's become somewhat of an unfortunate moniker.

Glimmer is intent on using every chance she gets." He smiles softly. "You can call me whatever you like."

"Hmm," I say. "Frosty seems fitting, especially after last night."

The King dips his head, color spreading over his cheeks.

"That's part of the reason I came. I wanted to make sure you were alright." His throat muscles tighten, but after a deep inhale, they relax. "Our dinner ended dreadfully, and I wanted to apologize formally."

I cross my arms over my chest.

"I don't think anyone cares to be magically tossed through walls and locked in their bedroom like some ill-behaving child."

Again, this need to nettle flourishes within me. Instead of getting angry, he looks more contrite. He brushes invisible dirt from his shirt and refuses to meet my gaze.

"I haven't been myself lately. It's not an excuse, but when the beast takes over—"

He breaks off in a fit of coughs, his powerful chest shaking with force.

"Because of the curse," I offer.

His eyes fly open as his coughing subsides. The King fists his hands at his side.

"You know about the curse?" Disbelief colors each word.

"It's obvious something is wrong here—things are not what they seem." I take a deep breath. "In my village, I was taught you were the one who cursed us and our land. All of our bad fortunes landed squarely on your shoulders. It's clear to me now that you may have had a hand in why this curse happened, but you were not the one who cast it."

The King nods. "You are right. I did not enact the foul magic that turned these lands into what they are now."

"Do you have any idea how I could break it?" I ask.

"I did once—now I've forgotten. It's been stolen away with

most of my memories." He grits his teeth. "Time is almost up. I can feel it. The five centuries I've been forced to endure are almost at an end."

My mouth goes dry.

"Five centuries?"

The King's lips pull into a smile, even if it doesn't reach his eyes.

"I wasn't always like this. Long ago, before the curse was laid, I was a powerful male fully in control of myself and this land. My only desire was to find—" He breaks off, eyes skimming over my face for a moment before shaking his head. "I can't remember now. Regardless, most of my power was stripped away instantly, and I became this. Barely in control of my body—shackled to this beast while my memories fade each year."

Stepping closer to me, our bodies nearly touch.

"The only thing I know is that I cannot help you break it. That was the one rule written into my bones when the curse was enacted. If it is to be broken, only you can do it. And if you don't, this realm will be plunged into icy darkness, and everyone will freeze."

I roll my eyes, huffing a laugh.

"No pressure."

The King gently settles his large hands on my shoulders and gives me a soft squeeze. I feel his warmth through my layers of clothing. Pleasure washes over me at the brief touch. I should've experimented with men back in my village. Then maybe I wouldn't be so affected by the minor grazes of this male. I don't push him away. I silently will him to pull me closer to him.

I am losing my mind, and I've only been here a day.

"When the sun is up, I will fight the beast to stay here with you. I want to show you the male I once was. Moreover, I want you to see my realm and why you may wish to save it. The more you learn, the more I can share with you." His grip on me tightens as his eyes grow serious. "But I'll have to let the beast out eventually. That is why you must promise me never to venture into my room on the third floor. I don't know how he would respond to you after I've suppressed him for so long, and I won't risk your safety."

"I wouldn't know how to get there even if I wanted to," I grumble.

His lips twitch. "Promise me you won't. No matter what."

I incline my head. "I promise."

Satisfied, he releases my shoulders, and I feel cold instantly. Turning my head, I gaze towards the window—the stone I used to guide me last night blends in with all the others.

"Do you think more secrets will be revealed in the hidden corridor?"

The King's brows lower. "What corridor?"

I wave a hand towards the window.

"The riddle you told me last night—I figured it out. That stone in the center is a key to release a secret door that leads into a hidden passway. That's where I found the necklace. Isn't that what you were trying to tell me?"

Dark blue stains his cheeks. "Truthfully, I didn't know the answer to the riddle. I could only remember that I needed to share it with you."

I nod, feeling a sense of pity. How awful it must be to know you are cursed—to understand how to break it—but to have forgotten it after all this time. Walking over to the window, I kneel before the stone. In the morning light it looks as ordinary as all the others.

"Here, let me show you," I say, reaching behind the rock.

Only this time, my fingers brush the wall before reaching behind the stone. I try to twist it, but nothing happens. It feels lifeless against my palm, not humming with power as before.

"I don't know why it isn't working," I mutter.

Soft footsteps creep up behind me. Looking up, I realize I am at eye level with a very intimate part of the Frost King. Quickly, I rise to my feet, willing my face to not flush. The Frost King's eyes are sad as she shakes his head.

"The secrets of this castle will not reveal themselves in my presence—only to you."

I try and fail not to roll my eyes again.

"Of course they fucking won't, Frosty."

Slapping a hand over my, I'm mortified. I never curse—Mama hates it, but I can't hide my exasperation after one step forward today and twenty back. The Frost King—Frosty, I shall call him because the formal title is grating on my nerves—widens his eyes before tossing his head back. A booming laugh echoes out of him, and I can't help but grin.

Amusement floods his blue eyes as he gently cups my cheek. I suck in a breath, itching to lean fully into his hold. His hands are deliciously warm and soft as silk. Biting his lip, he gently traces the hollow of my cheek.

"Why me?" I ask.

Frosty's eyes turn serious. His smile dims as he strokes my skin again.

"I wish I had a better answer to give. All I know is that from the moment I saw you, it was the first time I felt like myself in centuries. I felt hopeful." His fingers flex against me. "I truly am sorry for dragging you into all of this. This burden is not yours, yet I have settled it upon your shoulders."

Releasing me, he dips into a dramatically formal bow.

"Please, lovely Dove, allow me the honor of showing you my castle."

I incline my head as I watch dark blue dance over his cheeks.

"And," he adds, "because I want to show you the male I am. The real me. I want to wipe the memory of the beast away and have a fresh start between us."

Appraising him from head to toe, I bite my lip. I should tell him no—say to him that I have work to do if I am going to break this curse. The task already seemed overwhelming yesterday, and now it has worsened after learning what's at stake if I fail.

Especially given the fact that I have yet to figure out where to start.

Despite that, I let the idea of spending the day with him flood me. The thought is a pleasant one. Part of me is still weary of him—of the beast, as he calls it. Yet a more significant, more demanding part of me wants to learn who the real Frosty is.

As the thought occurs, the snowflake at my throat glows in approval. The memory from last night resurfaces as I remember the old Frost King's words. *The snowflake will guide you home.* Perhaps if I trust this magical crystal, I'll be one step closer to reuniting with my family before it's too late.

Frosty raises his brows at me.

"Let me change into something warmer," I say. "Then I'd love to go exploring."

13

THE FROST KING

The beast is sleeping.

Her proximity gives him the strength to keep it away. For the first time in centuries, he feels warm—like himself. Frosty, she calls him. That meddling snow fairy gave the nickname, yet it brings a smile to his lips every time she uses it. Walking beside her now, he can't help but steal another glance at her.

She looks beautiful. The pale blue of her fur-trimmed dress compliments the dark length of her hair. Her brown eyes glow with wonder as she takes in the castle. Little gasps of amazement heat his blood to a raging fire.

A delicate shade of pink colors her round cheeks. How would that blush feel against his lips? His tongue? Do other parts of her turn that delicious color?

Swallowing his growl, he pushes the thoughts from his mind. He can't give in to temptation—being next to her is more than enough—more than he's ever deserved.

The snowflake at her throat glows, calling forth old memories. Happy ones from when he was a child. Memories he thought were lost forever. He'll remember more soon—he has to.

For now, everything hinges on her.

He's being selfish—knows he should be doing a million other things. Preparations still need to be made, yet he is walking with her and willing the beast to stay away, even knowing the price he will have to pay for it later.

When Dove looks up with a soft smile on her lovely mouth, he knows the pain he will experience tonight will be more than worth it.

14

DOVE

Our walk through the halls is quiet.

Thankfully, the silence is not as awkward as it was at dinner the night before. Something unspoken rests between us. His plea to let me see the male he once was is latched onto my heart. The truth is, I want to know him—to learn who he was and who he could become. I want to understand what he did to have this curse placed upon him.

"My father, the first Frost King, built this palace as a wedding present for my mother." We pass by a crumbling wall where frost spreads like cobwebs. Frosty's lips pull down. "It was quite magnificent when it was well maintained."

"It's lovely," I say. We take our fourth right turn down another dilapidated hallway. "But terribly confusing to navigate."

Frosty chuckles, and the sound sends shivers down my spine.

"That's by design. It was built as a refuge for them. The magic woven into the palace keeps unwelcome visitors lost in its labyrinth. Give it time, and the castle will reveal itself to you."

His steps falter along the carpet. He turns towards me with wide eyes.

"I—I had forgotten that." Heat flares inside his eyes. "With you here, memories are unlocking."

I give a small smile. "I'm glad."

We continue our journey, plunging into silence once more. He glances over at me as I try to keep pace with him.

"What about your family?" he asks before flinching away. "Sorry, I shouldn't have—well, with everything—"

"It's okay," I say. "I'm happy to talk about them. If I break the curse, I'll return to them soon enough, right?"

An emotion ghosts over his features, but he quickly recovers with a nod.

"I have a mother and a sister fifteen years younger than me. She was a bit of a surprise to both of my parents, but Sophia was a gift. Papa got sick shortly after she was born and passed away before her first birthday." A familiar sadness clogs my throat. "I wish she could've known him. He was a wonderful father."

"I understand the pain of losing one's parent. I am sorry for your loss, Dove."

"Thank you," I say, blinking away my tears. "Anyways, we never had much—even less so after Papa was gone. But we had love, so much of it I didn't realize how lucky I was. Mama is caring and a phenomenal baker. Sophia is a thoughtful girl of ten."

Their faces swim in my mind, and I tuck them deep within my heart. I will be reunited with them again. I know it in my soul.

Frosty nods his head.

"You were fortunate to know such love. We don't know how lucky we are until it's gone," he says. His gaze darkens slightly. "Was there anyone else you spent your time with? Friends? Lovers?"

I wrinkle my nose.

"Mama, Sophia, and I lived at the edge of town. I didn't have much time for friends due to all the work needed to keep our small farm going. No time for lovers either, I'm afraid." I let out a humorless chuckle. "There were a few marriage offers from one particularly enamored man, but I wouldn't wed him. Not for all the silver in the world."

"Hmm," Frosty makes a non-commital noise while his face tightens.

My answer doesn't seem to agree with him even if he was the one who wished to know. We continue in silence until we reach a set of heavy doors. Each one has the standard silver snowflake adorning each door—the handles gleam as if polished recently.

The Frost King clears his throat before turning towards me.

"I wanted to show you this first. It was always my favorite room."

I watch as he presses down on the handles, and the large doors fly open. The breath stills in my lungs as I take a staggering step forward. It's a library. My village only had one meager book vendor that sold old, worn copies at a high price my family could never afford.

My eyes widen as I take in the wonder of this room. It stretches back as far as the eye can see. Long work tables with plush chairs line the center before tapering off into a grand fireplace surrounded by leather loveseats. A large painting of the Frost Mountains hangs over the mantel.

Marble with silver-veining comprises the walls and flooring. There are three levels to the library. Each one is filled with rows and rows of books, sparkling with the light streaming in from the wall of windows. I incline my neck to take it all in. All of this wondrous knowledge is nestled here—at my fingertips —and yet—

Frosty comes up behind me. I feel his warmth along my

back. I can't bring myself to face him lest he see the color swimming in my cheeks and sweat breaking out along my brow.

"I thought you might enjoy spending some time in here. Who knows? Maybe some forgotten secrets are tucked into the old tomes."

His tone is light—jovial—but it does little to relieve the lump in my throat. When I say nothing, he walks in front of me with lowered brows.

"Dove?"

I can't meet his gaze. Instead I drop my eyes to trace the sparkling silver along the floor.

"It would matter little if they were," I say, heat spreading down my neck and attacking my chest. "I—I can't read."

My truth lands at our feet, and I want to sweep it away—to hide. Mama and I never learned, nor did Sophia. Our village only had one teacher, and the price of school was too great for my family to afford. Papa could read some, but never enough to teach us.

An ugly emotion swims in my stomach, and I wait for the King's ridicule. He must be disappointed that the person he chose to help save the realm can't even spell her name. However, will I break the curse?

Anger burns through the embarrassment. It is his fault for taking me. I never asked to be his prisoner or his savior. If he is to mock me for—

A warm hand cups my face and drags my eyes towards his blue ones. They glow with sincerity—not a trace of pity to be found. Dark blue blooms on his cheeks and nose as I realize with a start he's blushing, too.

"Please don't hide from me," he whispers.

I swallow against my dry throat. "I—there was no one around to teach me. My parents couldn't afford schooling, so—"

"Then I will teach you. You're a smart young woman—

you'll pick it up quickly." His thumb grazes my jaw. "You're one of the cleverest people I've ever met."

I raise a brow. "How many humans have you met?"

A deeper shade of blue colors his cheeks.

"Well," he pauses, "none before you. But I know you're bright. And kind."

Despite myself, I feel my lips twist into a grin.

"In five hundred years, I'm the first human you've ever met?"

"I feel like it's imperative to remind you I've been cursed for four hundred and fifty of those years." He gives me an indulgent smile. "You don't have to tell me. I look amazing for my age."

A laugh puffs from my lips, the last vestiges of tension leaving me.

"I assume frost elves age differently than humans?"

"Slower." He gestures towards his face—nary a wrinkle to be found. "Clearly."

"Hmm," I hum. "Mama always said to help an elder whenever I could. I suppose that's what I'm doing now."

His smile shows off two rows of perfect, white teeth.

"An elder? You wound me. I don't look a day over three-hundred-and-forty-six."

His hand drifts lower on my cheek, gently skimming over my jaw and neck—goosebumps break out along my flesh. Being with him shouldn't feel effortless, yet there is a familiarity between us as if we have known each other for longer than a day.

Frosty's hands linger on the pendant at my throat. The longing in his eyes burns me alive.

"You don't have to," I whisper. "Teach me to read."

Determination settles along his features.

"I want to. Let me be the one to guide you. Please, Dove."

Not knowing what else to say, I nod.

Frosty inhales deeply, his eyes briefly falling shut. His whole body shivers as he slowly opens them. Their glow is so intense that it nearly causes me to lower mine. Dropping his hand from my throat, he drapes it along the small of my back and guides me towards one of the tables.

Nestling upon the upholstered chair, the Frost King waves his hand, and a blank piece of parchment appears. Next to it is a quill and a small pot of black ink. Frosty settles into the seat beside me, our legs brushing under the table. Awareness prickles my skin, and I try to still my trembling hand.

"Do you know how to spell your name?" he asks.

Reluctantly, I shake my head, tendrils of hair falling loose from my braid.

"Then that will be our first lesson."

Pulling the parchment toward himself, he gently dips the quill into the inkpot. Once coated in the black substance, he settles the tip atop the paper and elegantly scrolls four symbols. My name. It looks beautiful, even if the symbols—letters—mean nothing to me.

"Here, try and replicate each shape that I did."

Taking the quill from him, it fits awkwardly in my grip. My pressure is off, and my penmanship is shaky at best. I try to copy what the King did, but my work is a crude imitation. Setting the quill down, the two sets of letters couldn't look less alike if they tried.

"It's terrible."

A warm hand rests on my leg and gives me a gentle squeeze. Lifting my head, I meet his eyes shining with pride.

"You are trying. That's all that matters." He squeezes my leg again before pushing back in his chair. "Your grip on the quill is too harsh. Allow me."

He stands beside me and gently adjusts my hand around the quill. Fitting his hand atop mine, my heart races as he slides our joined hand over the parchment. Over and over, we spell my name until we need more ink.

My hand tingles as he gently pulls away.

"You try again," he encourages.

Slowly, I mirror the movements we've been through together. It is not perfect, but it is a vast improvement on my first attempt. The lines hold the same weight, and the curves are more elegant. I glance up at him and am rewarded with a smile.

"Wonderful," he praises.

Using his finger, he taps below each letter from left to right.

"'D', 'O', 'V', 'E'," he reads. "Dove."

I follow his finger, tracing each rounded edge and line while committing them to memory.

"'D', 'O', 'V', 'E'. Dove," I repeat.

"Perfect. My perfect Dove," he whispers before clearing his throat. "Next, we'll do the alphabet."

I nod, eager for more.

My perfect Dove. Something settles in my chest, a warm radiant light that tingles from my fingers to my toes. It feels familiar, though I've never experienced anything like it.

The sensation is quickly forgotten as Frosty settles in beside me, and I give myself over to the task at hand.

MY HEAD POUNDS as I brush out my hair for the evening.

I'm not used to focusing on one thing for so long. The King had been kind and gentle during his teaching. Nevertheless, he was a dutiful instructor. He made me trace over and recite the alphabet countless times. My hand began to cramp near the end of our lesson. We'd had to have been at it for a few hours while enjoying each other's company.

Then, in an instant, things changed.

After a powerful shudder turned his skin dim and cold, those feral eyes had returned. Gone was the warm male who gave me whispered praise and gentle touches. He was replaced by that harsh version of himself that dismissed me with a snarl, saying dinner would be delivered, and I was forbidden from leaving my room.

The nature of his curse is precarious indeed.

The beast was a stark reminder not to get swept up in his kindness. I'm here for a reason, and without indicating how long I have to uncover the nature of this curse, breaking it before we all turn into icicles is my most pressing concern. I cannot waste hours inside the library, stealing glances at the handsome Frost King.

Did he have to be so good-looking? If we're being honest, I found him alluring from the moment I saw him. Even if he did terrify me, his power calls to me, unlocking some primal part of myself. I'm growing addicted to his smiles and longing looks. Something I should not do as I plan to leave this place once I break the curse.

My heart aches at the thought, but it's the truth. No matter that when we are alone together, he looks at me like I am more glorious than the moon and stars. I cannot succumb to those lingering caresses even as I slip on my heavy wool robe, knowing that I'll be dreaming about his fingers after my adventure tonight.

What would they feel like on my naked flesh? Does he desire me in that way—beyond just someone who may free him from this dark magic? The heat in his gaze suggests so, but I've never been the best at understanding human men—let alone frost elf males.

I sigh and slide into my plush slippers.

The moon has risen, and the room is cast in a gentle blue glow. The window remains the same, while the stone I held the previous night sparkles again. Padding over to it, I gently reach behind and slide it from the wall. A familiar groan rips through my room as I watch the secret door open into the dark passageway.

Whatever I discover tonight will hopefully lead me one step closer to finding answers.

The snowflake at my throat flares to life and pulses in encouragement. Taking one last deep breath, I head into the corridor, the necklace and stone illuminating the dark path. It feels colder this time. I shiver and wrap my robe tighter around my body.

The wind blows through my hair and tickles the exposed skin of my legs. A distant humming sound echos down the hall. With each step, it gets louder until it sounds right by my ear. I wave my hand, only for it to connect sharply with a snow fairy's soft, plump body.

"Ouch! Watch it!" Glimmer snaps, rubbing her side.

I whirl on her.

"What are you doing down here?"

Ignoring my question, she flutters on her wings until she lands on my shoulder. Letting out a shrill whistle, she rubs her tiny hands together.

"You weren't kidding about the secret passageway."

I narrow my gaze. "I thought the castle's secrets would only reveal themselves to me."

Waving her hand, Glimmer gives a bored yawn.

"Those rules only apply to Frosty."

Shaking my head, I continue down the corridor as Glimmer lounges on my shoulder.

"If you must know, I was napping in your sock drawer when I heard the door open. I had to come see for myself what this place was all about."

"It could be dangerous down here."

Glimmer raises her brows as if to say, *Don't insult me.*

"If it's safe enough for you, then it's safe enough for me. I may be tiny, but I'm powerful." She waves her hand, and a glittering spray of frost covers the nearest wall. "See? That's why you need me. I'll watch your back."

"Impressive," I say, and Glimmer preens under my praise.

We travel further down the corridor, the temperature dropping the deeper we get. Glimmer burrows under my hair before slipping into my robe pocket for warmth. My breath begins to curl in front of me. Thankfully, we reach the end of the hall after a few more minutes.

This one appears to be in pristine condition. The double doors mirror the library ones I saw earlier, if only a bit smaller. Each one has silver snowflakes adorned with blue and white crystals.

"Wow," Glimmer says, popping her head out of my pocket.

"Do you recognize this door?"

The snow fairy flies forward and touches her hand to one of the crystals. Her wings flutter quickly before she floats back over towards me.

"Yes—but I don't remember why."

Tucking her back into my pocket, the necklace flutters at my throat, urging me forward. I reach for the handle, turning it only for cold air to cut through me. Unlike the one last night, this room is not empty.

It is a bedroom—a disgustingly ornate one at that. Silver furniture and bejeweled dressers dot every inch of the room. There are multiple love seats adorned with crystalized pillows arranged before a dormant fireplace. The bed is a thing of wonder—larger than the one in my room and covered in all manner of silks and furs.

Off in the corner sits a trunk peaking out from below a white sheet. I recognize it from the last memory. It was a part of Frosty's childhood room.

There is a tinkling in the air as a circle of light illuminates the massive bed. Resting inside the beam is a large egg the size of my palm. It is dark blue and adorned with silver jewels. It pulses in the light, radiating a power of its own.

Glimmer gasps and flies from my pocket towards it. She stops short of touching it, urging me forward with a wave. Her wings flap rapidly.

"I know what this is," she breathes. "*The Crystal Egg*. It is what the first snow fairy was born from. It was stolen from my people centuries ago. Why would it be here?"

I shake my head and reach for the item. As soon as my fingers graze it, the familiar sensation of being thrown through time shakes me. My body twists and trembles, and the world around me blurs until I land on my feet back inside this room.

Everything is the same, except for the bright light slipping through the windows. The furniture sparkles obscenely. Somehow, the sight fades as I take in the grouping of bodies moaning and thrusting on the bed.

My jaw falls open at the scene. There are five frost elf females scattered amongst the silk sheets. Their delicately pointed ears and glittering white hair fall over their bare breasts. Beside them are three frost elf males, two with shoulder-length white hair and one with hair shorter than the Frost King's. They expertly twist and turn, using their mouths and hands to bring each other pleasure.

I don't know where to look or if I even should. It's hard even to see what's going on with the amount of bodies. The sounds of coupling fill the room. The only noise breaking it up is a riotous banging outside the room. The sound never gives the bodies on the bed pause. They carry on until the door sounds like it is about to break off the hinges.

A white fur blanket flies off the bed, exposing everything and everyone, including the male at the center of the bed. He pulls himself away from two more frost elf females that had been hidden from view.

It's him—the Frost King. He looks younger than the male

I've come to know. The sight of him with all of these others makes my chest hurt. I rub the spot, feeling ridiculous. However, that doesn't stop the potent taste of jealousy from coating my tongue.

He has no claim on me nor I on him, but something about this scene makes me feel sick. Perhaps it is the cruel gleam in his eye, the one that reminds me of the beast he claims to be nothing like. Clearly, that was not always the case, as his skin is its normal luminous shade, and his hands are not tipped in claws.

"What?" he snarls towards the door.

It bangs open, and in walks an older elf male. Not the one from the first vision. This male wears some sort of uniform. There is disdain in his gaze as he takes in the scene but says nothing. The Frost King settles the sheet over his lap before snapping his fingers, and the two females at his side peel away and begin engaging with others in the bed. A goblet of wine manifests in his grip, and he downs it in one gulp.

"Sire, you have been neglecting your duties. The other lords believe—"

"Why would I give a fuck what the other lords think?" Frosty sneers, slurring his words. "I am the king. Kings do as they please."

"Your father has been gone for two winters. *Two winters*, you have been our king, and your realm has hardly seen you. You hole up here with your—your—" The other male inhales deeply to regain his composure. "I understand you are still grieving. Your father was a wonderful male, but—"

"Do not speak about my father," the Frost King grounds out.

"Your father," the other male growls, "would not want his one and only son fucking and drinking all hours of the day while his people starve. Not to mention the snow fairies, they demand to know what you are doing to locate their missing egg. They are calling for retribution on whoever took it."

A cruel gleam dances in the Frost King's eye. With a sinister twist of his wine-stained lips, he lets out a soft chuckle before shaking his head.

"Retribution? Demands? Who do those little beasts think they are?"

The other male's skin pales.

"They are your subjects, sire. You are meant to protect them. Whoever stole the egg must be—"

"Punished?"

With a wave of his hand, the sparkling egg I had seen in the room before manifests in his palm. Its power pulsates even in the memory. The Frost King gives it a causal toss before catching it midair. I grit my teeth at his carelessness.

"You didn't. Please tell me you weren't the one who stole it, King—"

"Of course I did. Those little pests can do without their prized possession." His lips flatten into a line. "If I am to suffer, so must we all."

"Sire," the other male calls. With a wave of the Frost King's hand, the egg disappears in a flash of blue light.

"You may go, Klause. I'm rather busy at the moment."

The Frost King tosses his goblet, allowing the fine crystal to shatter on the floor and paint the walls in red wine. He falls atop the shivering mass of bodies, and they lavish him with touches and kisses. Moaning ensues, and I have to look away from the wanton display.

The other male—Klause—pauses at the door.

"You do not know what you've done. Your father would be ashamed."

The door slams shut, and I am thrust back into my body.

The cold, dark room I left before comes into view. Glimmer is there, buzzing before me with wide eyes. Her little hands go to my cheeks and nose, pinching as she examines me. My head is swimming.

"What happened? One minute, you were here, but then your eyes went distant."

"Did you see the vision?" I ask instead of answering her.

Glimmer shakes her head. "When I touched it, nothing happened. What did you see?"

"A lot."

Reaching down, I gently lift the egg before setting it in my pocket.

"A good a lot or a bad a lot?"

I inhale through my nose, trying to rid my mind of those images—of the male I saw. How can he treat me with such kindness, yet that is who he is deep down? Is that the male he wishes to show me because I have no desire to meet him? That male deserves to be cursed for what he did.

My heart urges me not to be too rash and to give Frosty the chance to explain himself. What could he possibly say to justify what I just witnessed? A male filled with such cruelty like that should be punished.

"Dove?" Glimmer's soft voice is laced with worry.

"Sorry," I say, refocusing. After witnessing that memory, I know with certainty the first thing that needs to be done.

"We have to return this. Do you know where it goes?"

The snow fairy nods her head.

"The White Woods to the north. Inside the heart of the snow fairy fortress." Glimmer's color dims. "You cannot go there alone, Dove. The journey is treacherous."

I let out a humorless laugh.

"Oh, I won't be going alone. I'll be with the one who stole the egg in the first place."

Glimmer's mouth pops open.

"Who?"

Picking up my glowing stone, I hold my palm up for Glimmer to settle in.

"The Frost King."

15

———

THE FROST KING

He is caged within his own body.

The beast is loose, its senses much more heightened than his. It's why he can still smell her—her skin's rich, sweet scent lingers on his fingers. He wants to rip the clothes from his body and inhale every last drop of her from the fabric.

He wants to prowl the desolate halls of the castle until he can find the source. To consume her lovely scent until there is no way to remove it from his system.

Thrashing against his metal restraints, they groan but hold firm.

A necessary precaution, especially with her sleeping only a few floors away—tempting and unaware. He doesn't have much longer. Each day spent with her is a gift and a knife that stabs into his stomach. The beast demands he remember, but he happily forgets their impending demise.

Instead, he thinks of her—of her lovely face and curious dark eyes. It brings him comfort. The metal bindings will hold. There's no need to keep fighting tonight. He tucks away the vision of Dove into his heart.

He'll be ready to banish the beast come morning. For now, he must rest.

16

DOVE

I'm waiting for the King when he arrives at my room the following day.

I am wearing my thickest gown, made of heavy red wool that molds to my body. The neckline and sleeves are adorned with pale fur, matching the cloak's lining draped along my shoulders. Stockings cover my legs, and thick leather boots encase my feet.

White satin gloves cover my hands, and I can't stop wringing them.

A million questions swirl around my mind. I barely slept after returning to my room. What I had witnessed was enough to retrieve some dormant memories from Glimmer. The things she revealed to me had made my stomach turn.

There is a soft rap against the door before it swings open. He's here—Frosty—looking as handsome as ever. Dressed in his usual simple shirt and pants, his smile is easy as he breezes into my room. My stomach flutters at it, even if my face remains severe.

He draws up short as he stares at me. The easy smile melting away into a look of apprehension.

"What's wrong? What's happened?"

Worry laces every word. Crossing my arms over my chest, I shake my head.

"How could you do that?" I demand. "Take something so sacred to them."

According to Glimmer, the power and significance of the relic could not be understated. It meant everything to her people. Not only was the magic powerful, but it was also a symbol of where they came from—a rich piece of their history. For the Frost King, who serves as their protector and ruler, to be the one who stole it turns this crime into more than theft. It was a declaration indicating that the snow fairies were lesser than others under his rule.

It is an unforgivable offense.

Glimmer had said that returning it would be the bare mini-mum. She recalled her people's agony over the stolen egg, which many deemed an omen of their forthcoming demise. Then the curse came, and they all turned to ice.

The memory of the egg's disappearance had faded from Glimmer's mind until she glimpsed it last night.

Frosty's white brows pull low over his vibrant eyes.

"I have no idea what you're referring to."

Reaching into the pocket of my gown, my fingers graze the raised surface of the bejeweled egg. It hums in my hand. Even the snowflake at my throat dims in supplication to its power.

I extend the relic toward the King. His eyes widen, and his jaw unhinges. His blue skin turns a shade paler as he lifts a trembling hand toward it.

"I remember. I took it—but I don't know why." His eyes blaze into mine. "How did you find it?"

Gently, I tuck it back in my pocket, careful not to jostle the delicate egg.

"The corridor revealed itself again to me last night." I

narrow my eyes, and my lips curl. "I was shown a memory of you engaged in quite the sensual act."

The Frost King's cheeks darken, and he looks away. I continue, ugly emotions loosening my tongue.

"You were drunk and proudly proclaimed to your advisor that you had taken the egg. To punish those *little beasts,* as you called them. Saying that if you had to suffer, so too did they."

Frosty's mouth falls open, but he wisely shuts it.

"We must return it." I place my hands on my hips. "Now."

He nods his head, his shoulders sagging.

"Of course. I know where it goes. I'm...I'm remembering."

Brushing past him, I head towards the door.

"Good, then there's no time to waste."

I hear him fall in step behind me. I have no idea how to exit the castle, but my burning disappointment keeps me from asking Frosty for directions. Something heavy weighs my stomach down. He had looked upset at his action yet made no move to offer any reasoning as to why he may have thought doing such a cruel thing was necessary.

The vision last night had been horrible. It showed me a male that seemed in such contrast to the one I've come to know. At least he didn't deny his actions—I don't think my heart could take him also being a liar. It still feels raw after witnessing him with so many others.

My face feels warm at the memory. All those bodies, moving and moaning and—

"That male you saw isn't who I am anymore."

The King's voice cuts through the icy silence. He walks in step with me, guiding us down another series of steps and hallways. I bristle at his words, and my disappointment and jealousy force a humorless chuckle from my lips.

"No." I agree. "Just a cursed monster who steals from those he swore to protect."

As soon as I say the words, I regret them. The Frost King's

whole body rears back as if I've struck him. His powerful shoulders curl forward, and for a moment, he doesn't look like a powerful frost elf male but a small child.

I shouldn't care that I've hurt him. However, cruelty begets more cruelty, and I've never been callous. My hurt feelings have made me lose sight of that. Reveling in anger won't break this curse any quicker. As for the jealousy…I'd rather not examine why seeing him with those other males and females affected me so much.

It was long before my birth, and I shouldn't care, but that is easier said than done.

Pausing on the carpet, I turn towards him. I extend a hand and rest it gently on his arm. The heat pouring from him soaks through my gloves. His eyes lift, and I don't enjoy seeing the anguish I've put there.

I have not forgiven him for his actions, but that doesn't mean I must hurt him to express my displeasure.

"I—I didn't mean that. I feel foolish for—"

The Frost King turns away from me, my hand sliding from him.

"The only fool here is me," he says bitterly. "My selfish actions caused all this, and now I must deal with the consequences. I have earned your distrust."

I bite my bottom lip.

"Frost—"

"Let us go before we lose the light. It is quite the journey from here."

With a wave of his hands, metal swirls through the air, and we land outside. My boots sink into the fresh snow. It is only about ankle-high. Staying close to my side, I follow Frosty as he walks us towards the forest's edge surrounding the castle.

A few birds flutter overhead. The scent of fresh pine is crisp in the morning air. The breeze is cold, but luckily, the trees block most of the biting chill. I watch the green pines give way to white. We must be entering the White Woods, Glimmer informed me about.

Daring a glance at the King, his eyes remain focused ahead. Sunlight glitters off his silver crown. Despite the chill, he wears no coat. I shiver just looking at him.

We have entered into tense silence once more. Yesterday's progress is gone. Something in my heart urges me to speak, to make amends. The snowflake at my throat glows in approval, but what would I even say?

My disappointment has not gone away. Nor is it up to me to forgive him for stealing the egg. The King is right. His suffering is due to his cruel actions. If only his punishment hadn't extended to those around him. How unfair must this sorceress be to curse us all because of one thoughtless king?

Snow crunches under my feet as I dodge heavy branches. The deeper we walk, the quieter the world becomes. No more birds fly overhead, nor do small creatures scurry up trees. Only the sound of breathing and heavy steps break up the silent woods.

I feel his eyes upon me before he speaks.

"You are right," he says so softly I nearly miss it. "A monster —that is what I became. The death of my parents warped me into a cruel male who wanted the world to suffer as much as I did. To have the crown thrust upon the head of someone barely more than a child was more than I could bear. Unlimited power mixed with grief turned me into something ugly and wretched."

The misery in his blue eyes makes my heart ache.

"I drank and fucked away all of my problems. My people suffered for it. Now, even with the curse, a part of me wonders if they all may be better off. Safer to be trapped in their icy prisons than to live under the rule of such a monster." His eyes blaze with intensity. "I hate that you were forced to see that version of me—I hate that he ever existed."

The self-loathing in his eyes cuts me to the bone. Warmth unfurls in my chest and I will it to wrap around him. I understand the power of grief—to lose both parents and then inherit a kingdom is quite the burden to take on. It does not excuse what he did, but it does help explain why he acted in such a way.

"Why did you take it? What could the snow fairies have possibly done to deserve that?"

He shakes his head, white air flopping over his brow.

"They didn't deserve it," he rasps. "There is no good answer I can give—only that behaving cruelly allowed me to forget about my pain. Whatever reason I had at the time for stealing the egg matters little. There is no excuse for it, and if I could go back and change what I did, I would immediately."

I nod.

"You're making amends now. That is all you can do."

I want so badly to believe him. He's given no indication that he still carries those callous sentiments. Perhaps five centuries, subjected to a curse that's forced you to live at the mercy of the same cruel beast you inflicted on others has been a proper punishment. There's no doubt he's suffered. The only question remaining is if there is enough time to fix all the damage his actions have caused.

"Because of you," he whispers, breaking me free of my thoughts.

"Me?"

"Without your help, I never would've remembered just what an awful thing I did. This wrong never would've been righted. I've had centuries to do it."

"That's not entirely your fault—the curse had stolen the memory of it."

The Frost King shakes his head.

"I wonder now if part of me had wanted to forget." He blows out a breath. "For the first time, I'm considering if my true punishment was to force me to live in the world I was creating. One that would've been born out of my selfishness and neglect. I do not doubt that if I continued on that destructive path, I would be in a similar situation to the one I'm in now."

"You can't think like that," I say. "Nothing stays the same—people can change. What is the world without forgiveness?"

He gives me a sad smile.

"I'm not people, Dove." The King's hand ghosts over my cheek. "And I don't deserve forgiveness."

"If you truly wish to make amends, you do."

His fingers skim over my skin before falling away.

"You have a kind heart. If only—" He closes his eyes before picking up his steps. "Never mind, we're here."

Turning away from him, I stare at the sight before us.

A large archway made of glass and white crystal rises before us. It sparkles in the white light of the sun. Passing underneath it, the air hums with power, and the sharp sting of metal pricks my nose. It's eerily quiet. Not even the branches dare snap in the wind.

As we pass tiny homes nestled amongst the trees, our feet crunch along the ground. Each one sparkles brilliantly. The whole fortress seems to be covered in glittery, shimmering—

A gasp falls from my lips as I realize what's giving off the sparkling glow. It's bodies—hundreds of them. They are the same size as Glimmer, except they are made entirely of ice. Their tiny bodies remain frozen in their homes or lounging on tree branches. Some have fallen into the snow below, their wings spread as if they iced over mid-flight.

My heart cracks at the thought of Glimmer—this is her family, her friends—she's had to endure these centuries all alone.

"I haven't been here since—" The Frost King swallows loudly. "How could I let this happen? Look at them. They didn't even stand a chance."

Tears burn in my eyes, but I blink them away. Digging into the pocket of my cloak, I find the egg and hand it to Frosty.

"Then take the first step in making it right."

Holding the egg, he gently traces the delicate row of silver jewels. *The Crystal Egg* glows in his hand. Frosty lets out a delicate hiss but never drops the relic.

We walk through more snow, careful not to step on any fairies. Soon, we reach the center of the fortress. There lies a statue taller than even the King. It is made of dark stone, save for her wings, which are made of white crystal. A hood is pulled over her head. Her lips are carved into a gentle smile. Two hands are cupped in front of her, the stone in the center of her palms slightly paler than the rest.

Walking towards it, Frosty gently sets the egg back in her hands.

Nothing happens for a moment until *the Crystal Egg* blazes with life. Blue and white light pour from it and up the statue. The wings at her back glow in blues, pinks, and yellows—shimmering enough to sting my eyes. The King is at my side, half standing in front of me in protection.

"*See. Feel.*" a voice whispers through the trees and swirls around us. "*It takes one to see but two to feel. Hidden deep within the frozen lake, the secrets will reveal.*"

The glow of the egg dies down, and the wind relaxes into a gentle breeze.

"Wonderful," I murmur. "Another riddle."

Frosty turns towards me with a raised brow.

"I didn't hear anything."

"Of course not."

"We should head back." He glances towards the sky. "Those clouds mean more snow."

Above us, heavy white-gray clouds roll along the blue sky, blotting out the sun. Already, the temperature is beginning to drop. Looking over towards the statue, something kindles in my chest.

"Wait." Before he can turn, I snag his arm. "I'm happy you did that. Hopefully, it brings us one step closer to ending this curse."

His hand comes to rest atop mine.

"I didn't do it for the curse—I did it because it was what I should've done long ago." Dark blue blooms on his cheeks. "My motives were not completely altruistic. I wanted you to see that I wasn't at all like the version of me you saw."

"I know you're not." He looks unsure, even as I give his arm a gentle squeeze. "That cruel, drunk king never would've spent hours teaching me to spell my name. He wouldn't have cared to return the egg—keep showing me this Frosty. I like him."

My heart races at my admission. Even the King seems at a loss for words.

It's the truth. I do like him—more than I want to admit to. Sure, it's quick, but why wait to acknowledge these feelings if time is running out? I like how he makes me feel. I enjoy his company when he isn't behaving like a beast. More than that, I want to believe that the King I saw is not the one who stands before me today.

All my residual disappointment leaves me. This newfound bond between us deserves a chance to grow. If I let it, the path toward breaking the curse will reveal itself more easily. At least, I hope so. The snowflake at my throat hums, causing my lungs to vibrate. It is pleased with my confession.

"He—um—I like you too." His face is awash in dark blue.

"What's not to like? One day in my presence, you're already returning stolen sacred relics." I shrug. "Who knows what you'll have accomplished after a week in my company?"

He chuckles, tucking my hand in the crook of his arm and leading us from the fortress. I lean against his side as we pass under the archway. The warmth of his body seeps into me through my layers of clothing.

"It's still early," he says. "If you wanted to return to the library, we could—"

Frosty goes silent, and his whole body tenses. For a second, I think he is about to be consumed by his beast. The vein in his neck is pulsing, and his fingers have curled into claws. I do not want to be stranded out here with that thing.

I open my mouth, but Frosty pins me with a sharp look.

"Get behind me. Now."

I'm about to ask what's going on when I hear it.

The snap of a twig is followed by the echoing snarl coming from just ahead of us. The white evergreen trees fall back, their branches snapping as it makes its way towards us. I can feel the ground rumbling with each mighty step. Its glowing blue eyes emerge first from the shadows. Then, two rows of sharp teeth and a saliva-soaked red tongue appear. It walks on all fours. Its white fur-covered body is corded with muscle.

A bear, larger than any I've seen, stares us down. Its eyes lock with mine as it scents the air.

The Frost King slides in front of me in one fluid movement.

I take a slow step back, trying not to make a sound. Blue light tingles in Frosty's palms as the taste of metal coats my tongue.

"I will use my magic to take you back to the castle. I just need you to—"

A roar rips through the forest, sending birds and other animals scattering.

Its white fur blends into the snow as it races towards us with imperceptible speed. Its maw yawns open as it leaps through the air with claws and fangs extended.

17

THE FROST KING

The beast and him agree for the first time in centuries: save Dove.

He melted away and let the beast rise to the surface, ready to fight. The need to spill blood pours through his veins. All the beast knows is *kill, kill, kill*. To save her, he must succumb to this loathsome part of himself. He must give in to the primal urge to claw, bite, and rip apart.

It is the part of him she is repulsed by—she may hate him after seeing what he is capable of. It matters little as long as she is alive.

Keep her safe, keep her safe, keep her safe.

His hands meet fur and warm muscles. Blood spills up his arms and across his body, but he doesn't feel it. The sting of claws and bites barely registers to the beast.

Over and over, he fights it. Two monsters clashing in a deathmatch over the most precious prize. He will not lose when she is on the line.

The bear gives one final howl as he punches deep into its throat. With a tug, the meaty sound of flesh hitting the snow reaches his ears: the white bear crumbles, its fur stained crimson.

A familiar voice begs to be let out—for him to remember who he is—but the beast is in complete control.

He pushes it far into the darkness, where its pleading can no longer reach him.

18

DOVE

The scene before me is nothing short of carnage.

Puddles of red blood lie atop the snow. The bear is a pile of ripped muscle and broken bones. Its body hasn't moved since the King ripped out its throat. The squelching sound of it will haunt my dreams for years to come.

Now it is Frosty and I alone in the clearing once more. He merely stares at me, the feral gleam in his eye letting me know his beast is in control. The thick muscles of his chest and shoulders rise and fall with each labored breath. His skin is sallow—not the vibrant blue I've come to expect.

"Frosty," I whisper.

He merely blinks at me, his mouth opening to show two distended fangs.

"Frosty, it's me. Dove. You remember?"

A light sparks in his eyes. His shoulders sag, and for a moment, I hope the beast is releasing his control. Only to have it shatter instantly as his face twists into a snarl. His clawed hands extend towards me as he advances at inhuman speed.

I hold my ground, even as my whole body begins to tremble.

"Stop," I command. "You know me. I know you do. Remember who you are—the male you are."

He snarls again, his hands falling to my waist. Claws nearly pierce through the wool of my dress. Glowing eyes bore down at me. It isn't until my back hits the base of an evergreen tree that I realize he was moving me. I stare up at him as my heart pounds painfully.

"That male is gone," he growls, his voice lower than I've ever heard.

"No, he's not," I urge.

"I should punish you." His hands grip me harder. The tip of his nose nearly brushes mine. "You make him feel."

Lifting my trembling hands, I let instinct guide me. My palms cup his cold cheeks. He snarls but doesn't push me away. I feel the puff of his breath against my lips. A delicious thrill runs through me at our proximity. There has to be a way for me to reach Frosty—to encourage him to take his power back from the beast.

"Come back to me," I whisper, my thumbs smoothing over his skin. "I know you can hear me. Please."

The feral gleam burns in his gaze.

"Please, Frosty. Come back."

Licking over my lips, I don't let my nerves steal my resolve. It's the only thing I can think of that might reach him. Pushing up on my toes, I meet his cold lips with my own. Warm light spills from my chest even as the King's lips remain unresponsive. No matter. I have enough heat within me to thaw his icy exterior.

Pulling back, I kiss him again, harder this time. The snowflake at my throat erupts in white light I can see even through my closed eyes. Slowly, I feel the beast loosen his hold on me. His lips become more pliable until they gently return pressure on mine.

I give a moan of encouragement, unsure if I'm doing this

right. The last boy I kissed was at nine, and it lacked any sort of expert technique. Whatever I'm doing seems to be working as the coldness in his body melts away—his hands rover over my waist without any pricking of claws.

Frosty hauls me closer to him, our lips coming apart momentarily before reconnecting. There's an urgency to his kiss as if he can devour me whole. The rough trunk of the tree digs into my back. One large hand skims over my backside, and I gasp into his mouth. Using the opportunity, his tongue tangles with mine—guiding it with gentle strokes on how to kiss him back.

My head spins at the taste of him. I want to swallow it down and commit every part of him to memory. His muscles meet my soft curves. My breasts are crushed against his chest, and his seeking hardness presses against my stomach. A delicious shiver of pleasure rips through me as he hauls me more firmly against him.

His other hand goes to my hair, resting against my skull and tilting my head upwards. I never want to stop. Desire, something I've never felt for anyone, pours from me. This is a dangerous feeling, but I can't help but give myself over it.

Frosty tempts my selfishness. I let his kisses wash over me and forget what I should be doing. There is only his mouth and his tongue. My thighs rub together—wetness already forming between them. I'm desperate for any sort of friction.

His teeth snap my lip and give it a gentle nip. My eyes fly open as he trails open-mouth kisses along my jaws. His hands slip from my head and find the small of my back. He nips at my pulse, and my mouth falls open.

"Frosty."

He chuckles against my throat before skimming his warm tongue up my neck. I shiver as he presses one final firm kiss against my lips. Pulling away, the tree against my back is the only thing keeping me upright. My legs feel like jam. I suck down mouthfuls of cold air.

"Beautiful," he whispers, tucking a stray hair behind my ear.

My face flushes; the reality of what we've just done presses down on me. His clear gaze lingers on my cheeks as his grin deepens. Clearing my throat, I scan the treeline behind him instead of meeting his gaze.

"I'm glad you're, um, back." I want to smack myself.

A warm palm cups my chin and brings my eyes back to him.

"The beast is hard to keep tucked away. It takes considerable magic to do so—magic I'm quickly running out of."

I nod. "All the more reason I need to get to the bottom of this curse."

The King's eyes turn sad before dropping to my mouth. His thumb traces my swollen lips, and suddenly, I'm breathless again.

"Why did you kiss me, Dove?"

My face heats anew.

"It seemed like the most logical thing to do." I shrug.

Sadness frosts over his gaze, but he merely nods, dropping my chin. I immediately want to ask for his touch back. He steps back from me, putting more unwanted distance between us. Pushing off the tree, I stand before him close enough for our chests to brush.

"But mostly because I wanted to," I admit. "I haven't kissed anyone in a long time. I've never felt like this before."

A satisfied smile stretches his full lips.

"Then it was my honor to receive your kiss." He winks at me. "I'd very much like them bestowed upon me again. Several times."

I playfully swat at his arm.

"You'll have to do something to earn it," I tease.

When have I ever felt this comfortable around a male? In my heart, this feels right; it feels as if I've known him all my life. It is as if we are merely two beings meant to find each other— not doomed by some curse and forced to search for a way to break it before time runs out.

That cold thought threatens to ruin the moment, but I shake it off.

With a snap of his fingers, the blood is cleared from both of our clothes. Frosty dips into a dramatic bow, holding out his hand towards me.

"Allow me, my sweet Dove, the privilege of receiving another of your perfect kisses."

I smile at him before taking his hand. He tucks me into his side, and I immediately feel at ease.

"You can start with taking me back to the library," I say. "I'm eager to learn more."

The King smiles, and it's the most beautiful thing I've ever seen.

"Whatever you want, Dove. Always."

SEATED in the library with a fresh pot of ink, I trace over the three letters before me.

"What's that spell?" Frosty asks gently, peering over my shoulder.

"'H', 'E', 'R'," I read. "Her."

His blue eyes sparkle.

"Excellent work, Dove. I'm impressed with just how quickly you're picking this up."

As was I. We had been in the library for a few hours. My cloak sat drying in front of the roaring fireplace, along with my leather boots. My stocking-clad feet glide along the smooth tiles of the floor as I absorb his praise.

Frosty is an excellent teacher. He is patient and corrects me gently whenever I make a mistake. Even my penmanship has shown vast improvements. I'm farther along in understanding than I thought I'd be after just one day.

"Would you like to move on to a more difficult task?"

"What would that entail?" I ask.

Pulling out the chair beside me, he slides onto it with fluid grace. Suddenly the air is sucked from the room. His eyes dip to my mouth, and the memory of our frantic kissing in the woods returns. The memory heats my blood for the fiftieth time since we arrived in the library.

I clench my thighs together under the table.

"I'll give a series of words, each getting progressively more difficult." His eyes heat. "For each one you get right, I'll kiss you. As a reward, of course."

I raise a brow even as I feel my face flush.

"That sounds like more of a reward for you."

His smile widens.

"A mutually beneficial reward, then."

Despite my desire to feel his lips again, my stomach turns. I drop his gaze and stare down at my piece of parchment. Trailing a finger against the textured edge, I gently shake my head.

"I don't know..."

Frosty shifts on his chair beside me.

"Do you not want me to kiss you?"

My eyes meet his serious stare.

"N—no. I want that. It's just—I'm worried that I won't—"

"You've come far, Dove. I think you'll even impress yourself." His lips curl into a smirk. "Besides, I want you to win these kisses, so don't worry about the words being too hard."

I let out a soft chuckle.

"Then be prepared to have sore lips because I'm getting them all correct."

Curling a lock of hair around his finger, his eyes glow brightly.

"I never said the kisses had to be on your mouth. You'll get to choose the placement."

I remember the feeling of his lips on my jaw and neck. What will they feel like lower? Along the sensitive skin of my chest or even lower still. I hardly suppress my shiver at the thought. I'm getting ahead of myself.

Gripping my quill, I dip it in the ink and grab a fresh sheet of parchment.

"Let's begin," I declare.

"My eager girl," he whispers. "Very well. Spell 'sat'."

I wrack my brain for the letters before gently guiding my quill over the page. Once I have them, I point to each one and spell out the word. His smile is brilliant, and he leans closer. His warm breath tickles my lips.

"Excellent, Dove. Now, where would you like your first kiss?"

Being in control is appealing. It's too soon to label this thing between the King and me. All I know is that I want his kisses. I want to spend time with him and explore this desire that's manifested inside me for the first time. Jon Nine-Fingers made my skin crawl—made me consider a life of celibacy rather than take him as a husband.

It's as if all those years I spent guarding myself against his advances have melted away. I am free to explore these intense feelings with a partner of my choosing. I never thought the male I wanted to do said exploration with would be the Frost King, but life is strange and unpredictable.

"My mouth," I breathe as he nuzzles against my ear.

Pulling back, my eyes fall shut as I feel his hand cup my cheek and bring my mouth up to meet his. It is a feather let touch, the barest brushing of skin, yet my body is on fire. It is over far too quickly, and I pout in frustration.

"The harder the word, the longer the kiss."

I narrow my eyes at him.

"Give me another one then."

"As you wish."

For the next half an hour, we continue in this way. He gives me short words—two or three letters—and I spell each one correctly. Then he rewards me with his lips, which I'm quickly becoming addicted to. He presses them to my cheeks, my forehead, and both eyelids. He trails them down my jaw and returns to my mouth more than once. Each brush of them leaves me breathless and wanting more, as do his teasing touches along my sides and legs.

I'm a whimpering mess by the time I finish spelling my name.

"This is the longest word yet, Dove. Where do you want it?"

His voice sounds rough. After each kiss, his eyes darken as if something primal is trying to claw out of him. Is it wrong to say I relish watching it? Glancing down, I can see that I am not the only one enjoying this task. I may not have much hands-on experience with males, but I am not ignorant of what occurs during physical intimacy.

The thought of the two of us naked, fitting together, runs through my mind. These thoughts threaten to sweep me away, and I'm tempted to let them. I want him—it's as simple as that. Taking his hand, I place it on my chest. It rests just above the exposed swells of my breasts. My skin tingles at the soft touch. A growl rumbles through his chest as his fingers tighten.

"Here."

His hand skims over my shoulder before cupping my throat. White hair grazes my chin as he lowers his mouth to my chest. His warm lips kiss the tops of my breasts, and my head falls back. The gentle grip on my neck tightens slightly. My eyes threaten to close, but I force them open.

"Beautiful," he murmurs before kissing the top of my breast again. "Delicious."

He reigns kisses from my collarbone to the neckline of my gown. My hands find his head and anchor him to me. Wetness coats my inner thighs, and I squirm in my chair. It's not enough—I need more, or I'll die.

My left hand leaves his head to hook into the front of my gown. With a swift pull, the top of my gown falls away, leaving my breasts bare to the room. The air is cool, and my nipples instantly harden. Frosty's eyes blaze like two blue flames as he gazes at me.

"Cruel, wicked thing," he mutters before his hand slides off my throat to cup my breast.

He roughly molds one in his hand before attacking the other with his mouth. He teases my nipple with his tongue, gently biting it until my muscles grow taut. He lets it go with a pop and gives the other one the same treatment.

My mind races. Never in my life would I consider myself bold, and now I'm watching through half-closed eyes as the Frost King feasts on my bare skin. He pulls me closer, plucking me from the chair and settling me on his lap. His hardness presses into me, and I wriggle atop it.

He lets out a snarl, his eyes nearly swallowed by his pupils. I'm desperate for any pressure to relieve the ache between my thighs. His nostrils flare as if he can smell my desperate state. Giving my nipple one final lick, his growls against my skin.

"Last word, Dove. Get this right, and I'll give you what you need." His lips skim up my neck and settle against my ear. "Your sweet, little pussy is soaking me right through my pants."

I gasp at his words, nearly combusting from his obscene observation. There is no point in denying it—he can feel the evidence of just how much I want him.

"Please," I whimper.

His lips move at my ear as he whispers the word. Trying to

unscramble my thoughts and focus on spelling is difficult, especially with him continuing to shape and taste my breasts. I writhe on his lap, knowing I need the release only he can provide me. The pleasure that will only come if I get this word right.

Dragging the parchment over to me with trembling hands, I write the word. My penmanship lacks finesse, but I'm beyond caring. I need this fire inside of me stoked.

"'F'," I sigh as he licks my nipple. "'R'."

His hands fall to my hips and work me against his hardness. My eyes flutter close at the sensation.

"Keep going, Dove. Or I stop."

My eyes fly open.

"'O', 'S', 'T'," I read. He nips at my throat. "'Y'."

The King smiles up at me.

"Frosty," I moan.

"Perfect." His lips find mine. "Now, let me take care of you."

Without warning, he lifts me from his lap and settles me on the table. My breasts jut into the air as he kisses down my throat before tasting each nipple. I am nothing but a quivering mess. His large hands skim over my sides before settling at the hem of my gown.

Gently, he raises it around my waist. Cool air kisses my stocking-clad legs. Soon, I'll be exposed to him completely. While the idea is thrilling, something in me makes my legs snap shut. My heart pounds in my chest, and my face feels hot.

The King raises his head, worry swimming in his eyes.

"Dove," he says, placing a gentle hand on my knee. "Is everything—"

"Sorry," I say, beyond mortified.

I've destroyed this perfect moment for no reason. Here I am, already half naked, desperately wanting to feel him everywhere, and yet I am acting like a scared lamb. Will he turn away from me? Someone as old as him is probably used to partners with more experience.

"Dove," he repeats my name. His gentle tone makes me turn my head away.

"I—I'm sorry. It's just I've never done this before, and now I've ruined—"

"You haven't ruined anything."

His hands hook behind my back, and he gently pulls me up. Cupping my chin, I curse the tears burning in my eyes. I feel so ridiculous.

"I moved too fast—I'm just greedy when it comes to you. I'm sorry, Dove."

He reaches for the top of my gown, but I wrap my hands around his wrists. Taking a deep breath, I look up at him. My earlier apprehension melts away. I am safe with him—I trust him.

"Touch me—you're the only male I've ever wanted to." I place his hand on my breast. "I need more."

His answering snarl sets my blood on fire. The King teases my breast while his mouth devastates mine. My hands curl into the front of his shirt and bring him closer to me. Our tongues clash in a frenzy, deepening this well of desire inside of me.

"Dove." He whispers my name like a prayer. "Dove."

"More," I beg. "Please."

Lowering to his knees, large hands lock around my hips and drag me forward. My own hands help shuck my skirts until they are up around my waist. Air blows against the heated skin of my pussy. Frosty's hands go to my inner thighs and gently slide them apart, revealing me to him.

"*Fuck*," he whispers. "You're perfect here, too."

"Frosty," I sigh.

His warm fingers trace up and down my inner thighs. Goosebumps break out over my skin. He skims his nose up my flesh, inhaling deeply the closer he gets to my center. I feel his stare on me like a touch.

"Pink and pretty. Does your pussy taste as sweet as your mouth?"

I throw my head back and open my legs wider.

"Find out."

He chuckles sensually before I feel his tongue lick up my slit. With a cry, I slide my fingers through his hair. The metal of his crown is cold against my skin. I like that he keeps it on. To have a king before me on his knees, pleasuring me with his mouth, is a sight that sends hot shivers down my spine.

His hands go under my thighs and gently lift me. His mouth descends on my pussy. He gently kisses me at first before his tongue explores me fully. The expert muscle swirls around my entrance, dipping inside and tasting me. Moans fall from my lips as he works me.

Splaying my hands out behind me, I lift my hips to grind against his face. He chuckles, the vibrations skimming along my skin. His tongue finds my clit and gently massages it. A lone finger dips into my opening. It gently prods inside, once, twice, before being coated in my wetness and pushing in fully.

The stretch is decadent. My arms nearly give out behind me. Every thought empties from my head. There is only him and I in this moment. The pleasure waiting on the other side of this mountain may kill me. It would be a sweet way to go.

"My perfect Dove is delicious here, too. Sent to torture me with her soft sighs and tight little cunt."

"Please," I whimper

Frosty tosses my legs over his shoulder and palms my backside. His fingers mold it as he devours me. Licking and biting until every muscle in my body is tightening. My snowflake flares to life in a beam of white light. My toes curl, and my thighs clamp down around his head.

"I—I'm—I—"

"Come on my face," he commands. "Let me taste every drop of you."

His mouth is everywhere, biting and sucking. The sloppy, wet sounds from me echo around us in the quiet library. His hands reach up and find my breasts, gently tweaking my nipples. My head falls back, and I give over to sensation.

Fire erupts in my veins and licks over my whole body. I jump off the mountain and am awash in pleasure.

"Frosty!" I scream. It's the only word I know.

My legs are locked around his head as I move my hips up and down to grind out every last drop of pleasure. My arms give out behind me, and I fall to the library table in a heap of quivering muscles. Pleasure races through me, causing me to twitch.

I've never felt like this in my life. Not only am I relaxed and satiated, I feel...complete. Whole in a way I have never been before. As I watch Frosty rise from between my legs and lick my wetness from his lips, a fresh wave of arousal rolls through me.

He looms over me, taking in my exposed breasts to the skirts still hiked up around my thighs. My eyes shift to the noticeable bulge in his pants. I'm transfixed by it. Reaching out, he takes my hand and settles it atop his hard cock.

"This is what you do to me. Anytime I'm near you, this is your effect on me."

I sigh and give him a gentle squeeze.

He snarls before taking my hand away and threading his fingers through mine. Leaning down, he kisses my cheek and forehead before capturing my lips.

"That will have to wait for another time." His lips pull into a grin. "You know, I never liked that nickname—Frosty. But hearing you say it with my tongue buried in your pussy I may have just changed my mind."

I laugh before playfully smacking at his chest.

When he lets out a pained groan, I quickly sit up. Frosty coughs as a hand goes to his heart. The muscles in his body tense, and I know what's about to happen. The feral gleam in his eyes returns with a vengeance.

"Go, Dove. I need to return to my room, and I don't want you to see me like this."

Quickly righting my gown, I slide from the table. I pause before heading to the door. The King watches me with wide eyes as I kiss him gently, conveying all I need to with that brief touch.

"I'll see you tomorrow for more lessons."

I tuck away his soft smile into my heart and quickly turn from the room. My bare feet move quickly down the carpeted halls. For the first time since I got here, I have no trouble finding my room.

Ducking inside, I quickly shut the door and slid down the front of it. Across from me, the tall mirror reflects me, and I gasp. I hardly recognize myself. My lips are red and swollen. My hair is one dark tangle. My dark eyes glow with a hidden warmth over my rosy cheeks.

I touch my lip and remember the feel of the King's. The feelings inside me rise—as dangerous as sharp knives. I need to end this curse, for everyone's sake. My resolve to uncover the secrets buried here has never been stronger, yet I'm more conflicted than ever.

After what just happened, I can't help but think that breaking the curse may give me the chance to stay here with Frosty. Not forever, of course, but at least for a little while.

That's what I tell myself anyway.

19

DOVE

Something feels different as I lay in bed that night.

For one, the moon has been up for over an hour, but the rock below my window remains matte and pale. The air in the room also feels different. There is no metal tinge of magic; it feels stagnant. I roll around on my bed, trying to quell my unease.

If only Frosty were here, he could surely relax me.

What he had done with his mouth was a revelation. Thinking back to what transpired in the library has me turning slippery between my legs again. *You know, I never liked that nickname—Frosty. But hear you say it with my tongue buried in your pussy I may have just changed my mind.*

He has a wonderfully filthy mouth.

I gladly would've said his real name if he had ever thought of giving it to me. In fairness, I haven't asked, but when I offered up mine, surely that was the time to share it. Does he not trust me with it? Jealousy fills my stomach with unease. Did those males and females in the vision know it? Did he invite them to call him by it?

I stamp down those unwanted thoughts. There are more pressing matters at hand.

At last, a faint glow twinkles from the corner of my eye. Sighing, I rise from the bed, tightening my robe belt. The familiar rock glows differently tonight. Its blue is slightly off in color. Bending down to get a closer look, it also appears that the rock is muttering and cursing in a familiar squeaky voice.

I pluck Glimmer's shimmering body out from behind the rock. Her blue form deepens in color as she bats her eyes at me.

"I was only trying to help," she explains. "That rock won't budge."

Settling her plump body in my palm, I walk us back towards my bed.

"Maybe there are no clues to be uncovered tonight?" I offer.

"Hmmph," the snow fairy pouts. "I wanted to get a head start on them. There isn't much—"

"Time," I finish for her. "Yes, I know, but if this castle has nothing to show me, there is very little I can do about it."

Glimmer's color cools, and my heart aches, remembering the frozen bodies of her kind. How lonely she must feel. I tickle her round cheek.

"The egg has been restored to its rightful place in the fairy fortress," I say. "The King feels deep regret for ever having stolen it."

Glimmer's color deepens, and her eyes glow bright.

"I remember more now—it's been coming back in bits and pieces. He was a cruel male—callous and hate-filled after the death of his parents. His father had protected the snow fairies, but *he* saw us as pawns."

My lips curl down.

"There is no excuse for what he has done. The past cannot be changed, only the future. He wishes to make amends for the male he was—only time will tell if he is sincere."

Glimmer nods before snapping to attention. Her gossamer wings flap excitedly as she buzzes before my face.

"You must change his heart—that's it. *When the heart is righted, so too shall curses be blighted.*" At my confused look, she continues. "Essentially, any curse can be broken when the one it was cast upon has a change of heart. It's written into all our magic—even dark."

Biting my lip, I incline my head.

"How do I go about doing that?"

"You already are. Returning the egg was the first step. Just keep at it; he'll be a good male, and we'll all be free of this wretched curse."

I nod.

"Sounds easy enough." A yawn sneaks up on me. "Well, if that's the clue for the evening, I may as well get some sleep. I've got a king's heart to transform in the morning."

Glimmer snickers before settling back on my palm. Glancing over at the bed, I find a small velvet pillow and lay her soft body atop it. She throws me a grateful smile and snuggles down into it.

"Oh," I say. How could I have forgotten to ask? "Do you know where the frozen lake is?"

The snow fairy frowns. Crawling under the sheets, I lower my head onto a silk pillow.

"When we returned the egg, the statue gave a riddle only I could hear. *'It takes one to see, but two to feel. Hidden deep within the frozen lake, the secrets will reveal.'* I thought maybe you'd know what it meant."

Glimmer shakes her head in a sparkling spray of fairy dust.

"I'll find out, though."

I smile my thanks at her, but she's already asleep. Delicate snores sound from her tiny nose. Turning on my side, it's not long before I follow her into sleep.

THE FROST KING

Time is running out.

He feels it more acute now than ever. It's been running out the moment he brought her here a week ago. How could he have allowed this to happen? For years, he willed time to move quicker so that his suffering would finally come to an end. Now, all he wants is more of it—even if that wish is useless.

The beast roars to life every evening. He uses every available drop of his magic to be with her during the day. At night, when he is nothing more than jagged, rage-filled shards of ice, he thinks of her—of her kisses, her soft skin, the sweetness between her thighs. He's only feasted from her once, and it is not enough.

To have found her is a triumph, yet he yearns for more. That greed is the reason he's in this predicament. He knows it. He's burned too much of his magic to keep the beast quiet. Soon, there will be nothing left.

And what will become of Dove when he finally succumbs to his punishment?

DOVE

Things have been quiet since our trip to the fairy fortress.

The rock below my window hasn't glowed once. No more secrets locked away in the corridor—all I have to go on is what Glimmer told me about changing the King's heart. The little snow fairy has been most helpful, tirelessly searching for any sign of the mysterious frozen lake. Though in the five days since I heard that whispered riddle, I'm beginning to think it'll never show.

As for the King and I, well—let's just say things have been quietly intense.

Take now, for example, the two of us sitting across from the roaring fire on opposite loveseats. The small chapter book in my hands occupies most of my time until I feel his heated gaze upon me. Glancing up, our eyes meet, and my mouth goes dry at the intensity in his eyes. Frosty looks as if he could pounce on me at any moment.

I'd give anything for him to do it, but it hasn't been easy.

For the first time since arriving here, the warnings of time running out could not be clearer. Frosty meets me in the mornings and teaches me throughout the early afternoon. We share chaste kisses and gentle touches, but never much more. If he gets too carried away, the beast comes to life, and it takes him longer and longer to tame him.

I have not felt his mouth on my sensitive skin since the first time five days ago. I crave his touch—now that it's been taken from me, I want it even more. Each time his lips brush mine, I want to pull him against me until there is no separating us.

One glance at his fingers cools my heady desire.

The discoloration appeared a few days ago. He told me it was nothing, but I could hear the worry in his voice. All the fingers on his left hand have begun turning white, and the frost spreads further down his palm each day.

How much longer does he have? How can I change his heart enough to break the curse? A curse I desperately want us both free of. Frosty deserves a chance to make amends and live as a better male.

My heart squeezes at the notion that I may have just found him, only to lose him.

Slamming my book shut, I settle it on the small table before me. Frosty's eyes track every moment, a feral gleam rising to the surface before disappearing. The snowflake glows, and bright light illuminates the dim sitting area.

"What happened to the others living here when the curse was struck?"

Frosty's eyes ice over.

"Everyone in the room when it was cast froze immediately. The others living in my realm slowly froze over time." He shakes his head, his crown glinting in the light. "If only I could remember more about that day—of how it happened—I could've saved everyone by now. I spent months relocating their frozen bodies to the castle's basement."

Frosty huffs a laugh.

"I was ashamed to see them—I couldn't stomach it. It was a reminder of all of my failings."

Reaching over, I rest my hand atop his. He shudders, his eyes losing focus for a moment. After a sharp inhale, he shakes himself again.

"I don't think I was ever meant to end this curse. All this was just an illusion—tempting me with the idea of breaking it while knowing I never could." He grips my hand in his. "I think —I think I took you knowing that. It was my final selfish act in this world and also my greatest punishment. To know you, but not get to have you."

My heart gives a painful squeeze.

"I'm sorry," he whispers. "For not being the male you deserve—for letting my people down."

Moisture glimmers in his eyes. My breathing becomes painful.

"I wish we had met before all of this," I murmur. "Maybe none of this ever would've happened."

His hand cups my cheek, and I swallow my gasp. The frost-bitten fingers feel like ice against my skin.

"If anyone could've stopped me from becoming that wretched male, it would've been you." I shiver as he smooths his thumb over my cheek. "The freeze is beginning—I can feel it. Fighting back the beast has depleted my magic. It won't be long until I join the others in their icy prisons."

Hopelessness weighs me down. If this is not the mark of a changed heart, then I don't know what it is. Genuine remorse for what he has done is written in his gaze. What will become of me once he is gone? Sadness spears through my heart. I can't consider such things. Frosty still draws breath, meaning there is still time to fix this.

"I will save you, Frosty. Don't give up yet."

His smile is sad as he brushes his lips over my forehead. My whole body tightens—turning hot. I need him. Each moment I spend with him, the feelings I have only intensify. It's like I was brought here for a reason, not just to break the curse but to find myself and learn what I truly desire.

The Frost King has claimed my heart, and I gladly surrender to him.

"Come with me," Frosty says suddenly, rising to his feet.

I follow suit and stare up into his blue eyes. Our chests brush, and I remember his lips on my bare skin. A shiver licks down my spine, and his eyes glow anew as if he knows what I'm remembering.

"Spend the day with me."

"We spend every day together." I raise a brow.

"No," he shakes his head. "I don't know how much time is left, and I want to show you while I'm still me. You've only gotten a glimpse of the wonders of my kingdom."

Warmth pours from my chest and tingles my fingertips.

"I'd love that."

"Good. Let's take the fun way down."

"What—"

Before I can say another word, Frosty hefts me into his arm. His muscular chest presses against my side as my arms wrap around his neck. With a nod of his head, the windows along the nearest wall fly open, and a cold breeze swirls into the room. Without warning, Frosty sprints towards the open window, launching us through it with a hearty cry.

I scream as I burrow into his neck. The wind whips at my hair and tugs at my dress as we sail through the sky. Icy winds carry us, and the world is one white blur. I close my eyes, not wanting to witness us hit the ground.

"Open your eyes," Frosty calls above the wind. "I've got you."

Reluctantly, I peel them open and am treated to the most glorious sight. We curl and twist in time with the wind. It pushes and keeps us afloat as we sore over the dense foliage below. Frosty's hands tighten on me as I take it all in. The mountains loom ahead. From this height, I can make out their snow-white caps. Clouds peel back from the sun, and I feel its warmth press down on me.

I hold on tighter to Frosty as a laugh rasps out of me. It's magnificent—a sight I'll never forget. I glance up to find his eyes on my face. The emotion swimming in his eyes is too intense to name, but I feel it all the same—the warmth of it wraps around my heart.

A strong breeze guides us lower until I spot rolling heels. The stone tops of buildings can be seen just ahead. The breeze dissipates, and we fall through the air for only a second. Then, I feel soft snow break my fall. I squeal at the chill. Popping up from the heap of snow, I spy Frosty's laughing face as he shakes the snow from his hair. He looks younger—more carefree.

Reaching for me, he plucks me from the snow and helps wipe the snow from my gown. With a wave of his hand, a white cloak with silver trim appears on my shoulders. The inside is lined with soft fur. Frosty secures it firmly before taking my hand and leading me down the hill.

A quaint town comes into view. The shops and homes are all made out of white stone. They glitter in the sunlight. Just like everywhere else in this land, they are eerily quiet. Entering the town square, I try not to recoil at the iced-over bodies lining the street.

Each one is frozen during a mundane activity. Some are crystalized, walking arm-and-arm with their friend towards a tavern. Strolling past a window, I see a family of three all frozen around the dinner table. Even their food has frosted over, and web-like ice crawls up their walls.

Glancing over towards the King, he dips his head. How they have all suffered. This punishment was too cruel. Frosty deserved to pay for his crimes and cruelty, but all of these elves and fairies? Was their only crime calling this land home?

Surely, the sorceress must understand that her actions were just as cruel as the King's.

Squeezing his hand, he tucks me against his side, using a finger to point to each building.

"My father would only go to that specific tailor," he says.

Masse and Son's Tailor are carved into the stone building's side. The ease with which the words come to me now is staggering. The knowledge Frosty has gifted me with has changed my life.

My eyes linger on the frosted glass. Behind it, rows of fabric and work tables sit. A frozen elf male stands with a piece of rope draped around his shoulders and a quill resting in his hand. He is frozen while making alterations—a project that may never be completed.

We continue in silence, our feet crunching on the snow below.

"That used to be the bookstore." He nods towards another building. "That was the butcher's. His wife owned the sweet shop next door. It was my favorite place as a child."

He guides me towards it. The inside is still, with no frozen bodies to be seen.

"Every time my father needed something mended or my mother wanted a new book to add to the library, we would always stop by here before returning home. We'd drink steaming mugs of melted chocolate." His gaze turns distant. "Those were simple times—happy times. My parents were a beloved monarch. They raised me to love this land and to fight for my people. I have failed their legacy, and I fear I won't get to fix everything I have broken."

I turn towards him.

"Do not despair. There is still time," I say. "Glimmer has been searching for the frozen lake. Perhaps it is the key to—"

His fingers skim over my mouth.

"I do not wish to give into false hope. It won't be long now—

I thought I had days but," he pauses, looking down at his hand. The skin on his palm is entirely white. "I fear it may only be hours."

Tears burn in my eyes at how unfair this all is. I wasn't even given a chance to uncover the secrets buried here. How was I supposed to change his heart any more than I already have? What could we have built together, given more time?

He catches an errant tear with his thumb.

"Do not cry for me, Dove. I was shown one final act of mercy in all of this—you." His lips brush over my forehead. "If the curse is not broken before I succumb to the ice, I want you to find my horse. It has been spelled to return to your village along with provisions. Whatever's left in the castle, you are free to keep. My magic should hold and spare your family from any more hardships. This is my vow to you."

Sadness encases my heart in ice.

"Do not lose hope, Frosty." My voice is rough with emotion.

His lips twitch upwards.

"That infernal nickname," he chuckles. "Somehow, you make it sound perfect."

I meet his smile with a teasing one of my own.

"I'd happily call you by your name if you ever decided to tell me it."

Sadness flattens his mouth. His hand drifts to my shoulder, gently twisting a tendril of my hair around his pale fingers.

"I don't remember it," he whispers. "Another thing the curse has stolen from me."

The breath shudders out of me. The anguish in his eyes is as fresh as the snow around us. My heart shatters into a million pieces. How foolish I had been for thinking he did not want me to know his name—did not want me to call him by it. I can tell how much he cares for me. Why would he keep such a secret from me unless he had no choice?

My poor Frosty.

Pressing up on my toes, I meet his mouth with mine. In a second, we are fevered, fighting with teeth and tongues to see who can devour the other the quickest. His hands fall to my back, hauling me against him and his hardness. I moan against his lips, delving my tongue in deep. My hands curl into his chest, locking him to me.

We hold each other as if we could be ripped apart at any moment. His taste and smell overwhelm my senses until there is nothing but him.

"You are too good for me," he growls against my mouth. "Too perfect—if only I had time to do this properly. Court you in the way you deserve."

"I don't need to be courted," I whimper, kissing him harder. "I want to be right here with you."

He pulls back slightly as we catch our breath. My nose and cheeks ache from the cold. The feral gleam in his eyes sparks before melting away. His hands trace up and down my back before digging into my hair. Pressing a soft kiss to my lips, he grins down at me.

"I promised to show you my kingdom. How easily I forget everything when I am with you."

"Good," I say, tilting my head for another kiss.

He rewards me with it before tucking my hand in the crook of his arm.

"Come, I have much to show you."

And so he does.

We spent the rest of the afternoon flitting between the different shops. Frosty uses his magic to bring some of them back to life. At least enough for us to enjoy warm mugs of melted chocolate. The frost preserved most of the ingredients, and I've never tasted anything so decadent.

Strolling through town, the frozen inhabitants faded away, and everything felt almost normal. The bookstore had been filled to the brim with old texts. I could see why a female who loved reading as much as his mother enjoyed the shop.

The hours passed quickly as we milled about. We shared laughs and kisses. Everything was so perfect until Frosty began to cough. His muscles were drawn tight, and his eyes went wild. With a sinking feeling, I knew our time was nearly up. It wouldn't be long before the beast emerged.

"I'm sorry to cut this short, Dove. I've used a lot of magic today, and the beast is growing restless. It would be best if—"

A swift buzzing sound cuts him off. A glittering orb flies through the air before stopping between us. In a shock of blue light, Glimmer appears, her coloring as vibrant as ever. Her wings flutter at her back as she bobs with excitement.

"I found it!" she announces with pride. "The frozen lake. We need to hurry before it disappears again."

My eyes go wide as they meet Frosty's.

"I will accompany you," he says, even as he nearly doubles over from a cough.

"Out of the question," Glimmer titters. "I'm remembering more now, and I know the frozen lake will not welcome you."

Blue rises in Frosty's cheeks.

"Glimmer, I—for what I did to your people, I'm so sorry. If only—"

"We don't have time for that. Apologize to me once the curse is broken." The snow fairy flies towards me and snags a piece of my hair. "We have to go now. There isn't time to wait for it to reappear again."

"It's too dangerous," Frosty states.

I shake my head, touching his cold cheek.

"I will be alright."

He opens his mouth to argue, but I silence him with a kiss.

"Trust me. You have been a good male to me and shown me kindness. Taught me not just how to read but also about myself." I meet his mouth again, committing the feeling to memory. "I will do everything I can to ensure you get to show the people of this land the male I've come to know."

Frosty shakes his head.

"How was such a wretched male like me blessed to know you?"

We kiss again. His hands are seeking underneath my coat. He cups my bottom, roughly shaping it as I moan into his mouth. The world around us melts away. My heart hammers against my ribs, and I clench my thighs together to soothe the ache.

A throat clears delicately, and I remember we aren't alone.

"We have to go," Glimmer urges. "Now."

Reluctantly pulling back, I give Frost a brave smile.

"I will be safe. Glimmer will lead me back to the castle."

His eyes flash as he presses a hand to his stomach.

"Go. The beast is in a foul mood, and I don't know how long I can keep him away."

Appraising him one last time, resolve settles along my bones. I will break this curse—I will free all who are trapped here. With that decision made, I let Glimmer lead me deeper into the darkening woods.

22

DOVE

The path to the frozen lake could not be more treacherous.

The weather has worsened since I left Frosty's side and followed Glimmer's shimmering body in the woods. This indicates that the curse's powerful force is reaching new heights. The ice-cold wind lashes my face and cuts through the wool of my clock. Heavy flurries float down from the trees, deepening the snow at my feet.

Several times, I nearly stumble. To her credit, Glimmer keeps a quick pace, dodging the heavy snowfall. Her blue color has gone pale, and the thick fog obscures her.

It feels like we've been walking for hours. The light is quickly fading as heavy clouds cover the moon.

"Come on!" Glimmer calls over the roaring wind. "The storm's only going to get worse."

The snowflake at my throat glows brightly in agreement. If not for it, we would be lost out here.

"Hurry!" the snow fairy's shrill voice calls again.

My foot gets stuck in a deep snow mound. I pull it out with an icy snap. The bottom half of my dress is soaked and clings to my legs. Glimmer only flies quicker. I'm nearly running to keep up with her. Each deep breath feels like a knife to my chest.

"I don't have wings, Glimmer," I pant. "Can you slow down a bit?"

Glimmer pauses, a flash of blue in a sea of unyielding white, and turns back to face me. Her small mouth twists down, and her wings sag. She flutters back towards me, placing a cool hand on my cheek.

"Sorry," she chirps. "It's just—ever since I went into that corridor with you, I'm starting to remember. Shards of memories have started knitting back together, making everything much clearer."

Her body glows dark blue.

"Like the day the curse was laid."

Wiping snow from my eyes, I give her a puzzled expression.

"I thought you said you weren't there."

Glimmer shakes her head before urging me to continue at a more reasonable pace this time. The snow is getting thicker, and the howling wind cuts to the bone.

"I wasn't—but I remember somehow. It's like someone gifted me the memories." Her glowing eyes widen. "*The frozen lake will reveal what has been lost to me.* It is a legend among my kind. If you ever lose your way, the frozen lake will reveal itself to you. It reflects what has been and what could be."

"Does everything in this land have to be a riddle?" I grit out.

"Remembering the past and glimpsing the future may be the only way to stop this curse. The frozen lake only reveals itself for a few hours each night. We must catch it before it relocates."

I nod, wrapping my arms around myself, and quicken my steps. The sound of the roaring wind swallows up each heavy footfall. I say a silent prayer that I don't freeze to death before making it to this frozen lake. What more secrets will I uncover there? I hope it is the final one. I know the type of male the

King is. I've glimpsed his true heart and have seen the goodness in him.

Glimmer lands on my shoulder as if reading my thoughts, tucking herself under my hair.

"Frosty is different with you," she whispers in my ear. "Not the male I remember from before the curse. He was good once—with your help, I hope he can be good again."

"You said changing his heart was key. Though given the state of things, I haven't changed it enough."

"The frozen lake may still reveal what needs to be done. A curse as far-reaching as the one laid on this land must've had some other way to break it." Glimmer shakes her head, and her color dims. "I was there the day his father died."

I whip my head to the side and take in her sad face.

"Frosty's father was a wonderful king—kind and compassionate. He protected us snow fairies and gave us places of rank amongst his court. We even crafted his mate's dress for her coronation. Snow fairy lace is the finest in all the land."

Mate. The word pulses through me. It tickles something primal in me.

"He was injured on a hunt," Glimmer continues. "Frosty brought him to us and begged us to save him with our magic, but nothing could be done. His mother had passed a few decades prior, and his father wished to be reunited with her. The wound was too deep for anything to be done—our magic failed, and Frosty blamed us for it. He stripped us of our titles and remanded us to the fairy fortress."

"Oh, Glimmer," I say.

"I don't see that young, cruel male anymore. I see someone older, capable of change. With you by his side, our realm will be shaped for the better."

I smile at her even if my heart gives a harsh thump.

I've been so focused on my desire for Frosty that I hadn't even considered the implications of what our being together would mean. Did he want me in that way—take me as his queen? Moreover, did I want to be one? Not to mention, he is an elf, and I am a human. Do such pairings even exist? Our life spans are not equal—what would that mean for our future?

Questions wash over me and threaten to pull me into their murky depths. Uncertainty prickles at my skin, but I shove it away. There will be no future for us to navigate if I don't end this curse.

"Everyone is capable of change," I say to Glimmer. "Sometimes it just takes another to show you exactly who you are."

Glimmer nods her agreement before flying off my shoulder. Her blue body zips around the nearest tree, and I quickly follow suit. The snow is getting heavier. Each snowflake pelts her small body and throws her off balance. She pushes through until we reach a clearing in the trees.

"We're here," she calls.

My boots stomp along the snow until I reach a slight dropoff. The fog pulls back, and the air is ripped from my lungs. Before me is a shimmering pool of frozen water. It glows a deep blue, and its surface is as smooth and unblemished as glass. Dark clouds roll in above, but the frozen lake remains calm. Snow piles up along the edge where we stand.

I look to Glimmer for guidance.

"Open your heart and feel it—taste the magic on your tongue, feel the breeze in your hair, and let it guide you to what you need to see."

I take a deep breath and fall to my knees at the lake's edge. Cold bites into my skin. The snowflake flares to life before me, and the lake reflects the harsh glow. Leaning forward, I reach for the surface of the lake. Ice bites into my fingers.

The warmth in my chest unfurls, and something else sparks in my mind for the first time. A golden thread, the end of which is obscured by darkness. Am I meant to follow it? The snowflake flares to life. Metal coats my tongue and slides down my throat. I reach for that pulsing thread and allow the magic of the frozen lake to overtake me.

It is a more gentle experience than the other memories I have been cast into. Instead of being tossed and yanked through time, I am simply lowered into the vision. At first, only darkness and the faint sound of music drift towards me. Then, as if waking up from a dream, the world around me swirls into focus.

I am at a glittering ball inside Frosty's castle. Dozens of frost elves are there, dressed in decadent finery. Their heavy ball-gowns sag under the weight of their jewels. Males are dressed in silk pants and coats ranging from white to dark blue. Silver trims each outfit, and they all sparkle under the candlelight. They dance with elegance as a large band plays silver embell-ished instruments. They are all smiling, but none of it reaches their eyes.

Ice sculptures decorate the room, each surface polished and adorned in finery. The scent of cinnamon and roasting meat tickles my nose. I glance to the side and see long tables of steaming food. No one seems to be eating it, and I have the impression that it will go to waste.

The opulence is repulsive.

No one notices me in my sopping wet dress as I stand in the middle of the floor. Despite the countless roaring fires, the scene feels cold. Raising my head, I finally see him. The Frost King lounges on a massive silver throne. A goblet of wine rests in his hand while nude bodies linger around him. He pays them little mind and snaps his fingers for his cup to be refilled.

Having learned about his tragedy, I can see the pain in his eyes. Grief turns us into monsters. I might've been just like him if I did not have Mama or Sophia. Nothing can replace the ones you love. This opulent display is proof of that.

A loud clap of thunder shakes the room. Glasses slip from the patrons' hands and shatter on the floor. The ice sculpture of a large snowflake cracks in half and breaks against the marble. Snow falls furiously outside the window. Lightning cuts through the heavy white clouds. A few elves give loud gasps and back away from the floor.

I glance up at Frosty, who narrows his bleary eyes.

"What is the meaning of all of this?" he growls.

Suddenly, the doors fly open and hit the walls with a loud bang. A freezing wind blows into the room, chilling even me. Frost crawls and cracks up the side of each wall, coating everything in a thin layer of ice. The storm rages outside, and a figure appears in its center.

She is dressed head to toe in white. Her cloak and skin glow, and her blue skin glimmers in the light as if she were made of ice. Her eyes shine like two blue flames, and long blue hair floats around her slender shoulders. Her beauty is fearsome.

The figure floats into the room. She is barely taller than me but somehow manages to suck the power from it. Raising a delicate hand, she extends a finger towards the King.

"You," she snarls in a voice that is soft and rough at the same time. "I know what you've done. For what you have taken, I now shall take from you."

Frosty's lips pull into a sneer as he scoffs at her. Rising from his throne, he tosses his goblet and descends towards her.

"Be gone, Witch. I do not care for these games."

Blue light glimmers in his palm, but as he waves it, the female remains precisely where she is.

"I am more powerful than you, young king." Her smile is cruel. "Perhaps you need a reminder of that."

Crooking a finger at him, the King flies through the air with a surprised grunt. He lands before her as shackles made of ice crack through the marble floor and lock around his feet. His eyes flash with bewilderment as he thrashes in place.

"Release me, you—"

"I am the Sorceress of the White Woods, protector of the

snow fairies, and keeper of these lands. For your callous treatment of my children, I have come to deliver your punishment."

"Unhand me at once, or I'll—"

The sorceress laughs delicately before waving her hand. An invisible force sends the King to his knees. He stares up at her with hot rage. Plucking the silver crown from his head, she holds it between her two palms. White light flows from her arms and over the silver.

"I curse you, young king. You will live a lonely life. Those in this kingdom will freeze and turn to ice so they no longer suffer under your rule. My magic will keep them blissfully unaware and protected by time. One day, you will join them in their icy prison, but not before you have suffered for the pain you've caused. You have behaved like a beast, and so too shall you be tormented by one. A restless soul will bind itself to yours and turn you into a snarling creature. A monster will grow in your heart until it eats away at every last miserable shred of you."

The Frost King stops struggling, his hands beginning to tremble. The thick scent of metal nearly chokes me.

"Do not despair yet, young king. For there is a way to save yourself. One will come who may free you from this curse—you will know her well. She is who you've been searching for since you were small. Your *mate*."

The Frost King bares his teeth. "You wretched—"

"Mating bonds are so sacred to your kind. It would be unfair for me to neglect it." Her lips twist into an even harsher smile.

The sorceress leans down and whispers something in his ear. I cannot hear it, but whatever she says makes his skin pale. The last of his fight leaves him, and he curls forward.

"Now you know what must be done for her to free you. Only you will be privy to this knowledge." Throwing her head back, she cackles. "But that is too easy. I want you to feel the same hopelessness my children have felt since you banished them. And that is why the thing you've used to hurt so many will now be your permanent chains. It will blight your memory —erode who you are until you can't even remember yourself."

"Impossible! If you make me forget, how will—"

But the sorceress merely gives another hearty laugh before she slams the crown down atop his head. Silver light pours from his head as the crown fuses with his skull—the Frost King shrieks and howls. Icy claws rip through my heart at the display.

With a wave of her hand, the sorceress sends a blast of ice to cover the room. The walls are leached of color and turn into the familiar white stone I'm used to seeing. Elves scream and try to flee the room, but it is useless. Their bodies are quickly coated in frost, and they solidify in moments.

The room goes utterly silent. At long last, the Frost King grunts and blinks, opening his eyes. Watching him take in the room, I glimpse the feral gleam in his eyes. With a sinking stomach, I watch as sharp claws slice through the ice around his feet. His lips pull back at the sorceress, but she twists into a pile of sparkling fairy dust and is carried off on a winter breeze.

The Frost King turns towards me. He is so close I can smell his pine scent. I remind myself that I'm not here; this is a memory, and nothing can touch me. Yet, I watch as his whole body stiffens and his nostrils flare. Reaching a clawed hand towards me, it nearly brushes my shoulder when—

Beneath me, the floor shifts, and I am gently pulled through it. The memory dissipates, and I am left breathless. Questions bang around inside my head, but I don't have time to consider them. Not as I'm thrust into another memory.

My feet land on the library floor. The sun shines through the massive windows. Before me is one of the loveseats, a pile of thick books stacked to the side. A dark-haired woman rests on the seat. I walk around to the front, the fire from the lit hearth licking up my side.

Once I am standing before her, the breath freezes in my lungs. The woman—the female—is me. Holding a heavy leather-bound book in her lap, she sits with her feet tucked underneath her. Our matching snowflake necklaces rest at our throats. Delicately pointed ears poke out from under her unbound hair. Sparkling brown eyes look up from the page and directly at me.

I hold my breath before she adjusts, reaching over to set the book atop the stack beside her. My mouth goes dry as I take in her—my—round stomach. It is proudly on display in her simple blue dress.

The nearest window clicks open, and a cool breeze blows in, bringing in a familiar figure. It is the Frost King, broader of shoulder and older. No crown decorates his brow, and he is dressed in a simple black cloak. Twisting in her seat, a warm smile breaks out across her face.

"You're back early, my love."

My love. Awareness prickles at my fingertips.

The Frost King settles in next to her and kisses her temple. Pink highlights her cheeks as his hand goes to her stomach.

"I hate being away from you, especially in your condition." He bestows another kiss. "How are you and our little one doing?"

Her hand comes down on top of his.

"Perfectly well. She's sleeping for now."

"Hmm," Frosty hums. "We still need to decide on a name for her."

The female elf version of me chuckles, snuggling deeper into the Frost King's side. The affection in their simple touches causes a wave of longing to wash over me. What a contrast this scene is to the one I just witnessed.

"Our sons are already named after you." My eyes widen. "Surely, our little female should be named after her mother."

The Frost King nods, pressing a gentle kiss on her lips.

"Whatever my mate wants, she shall have."

The blood freezes in my veins. This cannot be—I'm—

A loud bang echoes through the library as the doors fly open. An older male elf comes strolling in. He is lean and long-legged, the way most teenagers are. Beneath his crop of dark hair and matching eyebrows is a pair of sparkling blue eyes. Racing in beside him is a younger male who barely reaches his hip.

He is a perfect replica of his father.

"Mama, can we go into town?" the younger one asks, coming to stand before her.

Tucking a wildly curling piece of white hair behind his arched ear, she nods.

"Only if you wear your warmest coats, my darlings."

The older boy comes to the Frost King's side with a bemused expression. Love pours from the scene before me. It warms a frozen part of me I didn't even know existed. That golden thread I saw earlier is wrapped around the Frost King's wrist and tethered to mine. The snowflake glows at our throats, and everything clicks into place.

One to see, but two to feel. I understand the riddle now. Everything is clear to me. The memory—the vision of a future I may have already lost—disappears around me. The library's warmth melts away, and I am thrust back into the raging blizzard at the edge of the frozen lake.

My breaths are painful, and my body feels frozen. Rising on rigid muscles, Glimmer buzzes before me with wide eyes. Words spill from my lips before she can even ask.

"I watched it—the sorceress laid down the curse but left a way to break it." Tears sting in my eyes. "Only the king knows how. She told him before stealing his memory."

I give a heartbroken laugh.

"The only way to break it is lost, Glimmer." The snow fairy sags. "The sorceress made sure of that. I don't know if there is enough time to unlock the memories buried within him."

I want to scream and rage—to find this sorceress and demand more answers, even if it is pointless. Was all this indeed for nothing? My heart cracks down the middle.

What's even crueler is showing me the vision of the life we could've had. If only I had been born an elf—we could've met and had time together. I could've been there for him in his grief and stopped him from turning into the male who brought down this plight.

I think of Mama and Sophia, and though I'd never choose not to know them, is it wrong to want both? To want my elven life with Frosty while also keeping my human family? Those desires matter little now. Both may be already lost to me.

It was one final cruel twist of fate. Dangling the family and companionship I've come to desire before me, only to rip it away.

Glimmer's body is wracked with shivers. For the first time, I notice just how pale she looks. Her sparkle is fading quickly. She's too weak to speak.

"While there is still time, I will search for more clues, Glimmer. I will do everything I can with however much time I have to do it," I vow. "Now, let's get out of this storm."

Glimmer nods, a shimmering tear falling from her eyes as she turns and leads me from the frozen lake. Her wings barely hold her up as we pass through the White Woods, and each pelt of snow weighs down her body. The wind picks up as the trees thin, indicating we are approaching a clearing.

Up ahead, I can see the sharp spires of the castle. Relief floods me, thinking of the warm fire awaiting Glimmer and I. Glimmer. Her blue body is not in front of me. It was there one moment and gone the next. A fresh downpour of snow hinders my vision.

"Glimmer!" I call over the rising wind. "Glimmer!"

I turn in circles as my clothes become soaked. My feet can barely stop upright on the ice. My eyes scan the white waste for any sign of her. Then I spot it, her curvy form resting atop a snow mound. Frost licks up her skin, and I quickly grab her.

Jagged breaths rasp out of her lungs. The warmth of my hands does nothing to eradicate her chill. She has little time, and only one male can save her. This curse has taken so much from everyone here, but I will not let it take Glimmer, too—not yet, at least.

Tucking her shaking body into my chest, I heft my legs through the snow. The castle gets closer. I know the King has warned me about seeking him out at night, but I don't care. I'd rather take on the beast than lose my littlest friend.

23

DOVE

Bursting through the castle's front doors, I pause with Glimmer's fading body in my hands.

Frosty told me where his room was, but I have no idea how to get there. The snowflake at my throat hums to life, and I watch it lift off my skin and into the air. I don't have time to be shocked or even question it. Allowing it to tug me up the first set of stairs, I follow it, knowing in my heart that it's taking me exactly where I need to go.

The journey up to the third floor is a long one. All the while, Glimmer grows colder and weaker in my hand. Her lips have frosted over, and her wings no longer shimmer. I quicken my steps as the snowflake glows with more urgency. We take sharp turns down desolate hallways and the steps two at a time before finally reaching a landing.

It's eerily silent, but I can feel a presence lurking here.

The snowflake pulls me until I am standing before two massive double doors. I recognize them from a vision with their jewel-encrusted snowflakes adorning their surfaces. Pushing open the doors, I find the room barren. The furniture has all been covered with sheets and coated in frost. A fire roars to life at our entry, and I quickly set Glimmer down before it. Her eyes have fallen shut, and I swallow the lump in my throat.

"I'm going to get help. Hold on for me."

There is another set of doors towards the back of the massive room. I know what is behind them. The heavy breathing seeps from underneath the door, as does the faint rattling of chains. I straighten my spine and take a calming breath. I have returned Frosty from the beast before and can do it again. Walking over, I feel the cool metal settle against my palms and twist the handle.

An icy breeze rips through me.

Even the snowflake at my throat has dimmed its glow. The spacious room is empty. What was once a large bed has been shredded into splitters. Feathers litter the ground from the torn-apart pillows. Sheets hang in ribbons off the side and decorate the floor. Large, deep slashes cut through the wood paneling of the walls. Shattered glass and ice coat the floor.

A low growl lifts my gaze as I take him in.

The Frost King—or at least his body—is here. His eyes are feral—the pupils are nearly swallowing the blue. He is shirtless, clad only in simple pants. The corded muscles of his chest and arms flex as my scent hits him. He bares his sharp fangs, thrashing against the chains wrapped around his waist and wrists. Dread turns my stomach, but I won't be deterred.

Coming into the room, I straighten my spine.

"What are you doing in here?" he spits.

Those cold, unfeeling eyes rove over me.

"It's Glimmer—she's been hurt. I need your—"

"You know better than to come near me when I am like this. You should fear me."

I shake my head. "I don't."

"Foolish girl," he snarls. "I will be your destruction. I am a monster, and it's time you saw me as such. Free me from these chains, and I'll show you."

A shiver runs down my spine, but I shake it off. I walk closer to him, slowly eating up the space between us.

"I'm not scared of you," I say firmly. "This is just the curse talking."

His head rears back. "You do not know—"

"There is much I've come to learn about you since I arrived. I know the type of male you are, and this is not it. You are kind and gentle—compassionate. That is the type of male you are to me—one who is remorseful and capable of change." I lick over my lips. "The type of male I've come to care for."

His eyes flash as I settle my hands on his bare chest. I feel the hammering of his heart against my palm, and his warmth flows up my arm. I stare into his feral eyes and lay the truth bare.

"The male who is my mate."

His eyes widen, and a shudder racks his whole body. Yanking against the chain, they groan as the feral look in his eyes intensifies. The stone wall behind him crumbles, but I don't retreat.

"You won't hurt me," I whisper. "Please come back. Help me save Glimmer before it's too late. Please."

His whole body tenses as he lets out another snarl. The cursed crown atop his head glints as he thrashes. I watch the muscles in his neck twitch as he shakes from side to side. The struggle inside of him plays out before my eyes. The chains behind him pull from the wall. They slip from his wrists and waists, landing on the floor with loud clangs.

My breath catches as he goes wholly still.

Finally, he blinks clear blue eyes open at me. His skin is a shimmering blue, and his hands are free of their deadly claws. He stares at me for a moment, mouth slightly open. With flaring nostrils, he comes to life and crushes me against his chest. I bask in his pine scent, of the warmth of his body, even if he, too, feels colder than I would like.

There is still time to fix what has been done, but for now, Glimmer needs us. Once she is mended, I will do everything possible to uncover this missing piece. Frosty's heart pounds in a steady rhythm against me. We both deserve a chance at the loving future I saw. In his arms, I feel closer to that vision than ever before.

"My beautiful mate," he murmurs into my hair. "I've waited centuries for you. Even when I had forgotten what I was waiting for, I still knew you on that platform. I knew you belonged to me, and I belonged to you. It was why I chose you —my one final selfish act."

"I'm glad you picked me." My words are muffled against his chest. "There's so much I have to tell you."

As I open my mouth to reveal all I've learned, the words stick in my throat. Air rasps out of me, and I realize that the curse has affected my ability to share what I know. That sorceress is beyond cruel. Shaking my head, I look up at him.

"That will have to wait. Glimmer needs us." My grip on him tightens. "But I will break this curse, Frosty. For all of us."

He smiles, but it does not reach his eyes. Taking my hand, I am pleased to see the frost has not traveled further up his hands. That gives me hope I still have a bit longer to solve this.

Entering the other room, the Frost King kneels beside Glimmer's shaking body. Her breathing is becoming weaker, barely more than a puff of air. He trails a finger down her chest, and she doesn't stir. Shaking his head, he looks up at me.

"I don't have much magic left, but I will save her. This is my promise to you, Dove."

I nod and watch as blue, healing light pours from his hand. It encases Glimmer's body. Gritting his teeth, Frosty pours more into her. Slowly, her color deepens. Her wings regain fullness, and her chest rises and falls steadily. Magic coats the air as every last drop he can manage is used on Glimmer.

Finally, the blue light dissipates, and Glimmer sparkles

once more. Her eyes do not open, but her breathing is normal. I look to Frosty, who grits his teeth and staggers to his feet. He sways for a moment, and I come to his side. I swallow my gasp as I glimpse his hands, now white to the middle of his forearms.

Hopelessness rises within me, but I shove it away and burrow into the male at my side.

"She will live. She just needs rest," he whispers, sounding out of breath.

The toll this must have taken on him is great. He leans further against me, and I do my best to help support his massive body.

"Thank you," I say, kissing the soft skin of his chest.

After a few moments, he regains his strength and leans off me. I immediately miss the feeling of his body. The weight of the evening settles down on me, and suddenly I feel exhausted. A yawn slips from my lips.

Frosty takes my hand in his pale one.

"Come, you need rest as well."

I allow him to lead me out of the room, comforted that Glimmer will be alright. We walk further down the hallway until we reach an unfamiliar door adorned with gold snowflakes.

"These are the king's rooms. I haven't been in them since—" he breaks off, and I gently squeeze his hand.

Quietly, he leads me inside. Much like all the other rooms, white sheets cover the furniture. Gently, he pulls one off the bed before wiping away the frost and dust. The fireplace roars to life and licks over my skin. The cold room warms quickly until my heavy clock feels too hot. I untie it and let it pool to the floor at my feet before toeing off my leather boots.

Frosty's eyes rove over me, and anticipation kindles in my stomach. Reaching for the laces of my gown, I undo them until the garment slips from my body. I stand only in my thin shift and stockings, but Frosty's gaze never leaves my face.

"You should chain me back up," he whispers. "I don't know how much longer I can keep the beast back."

I simply shake my head, walking on quiet feet towards the side of the bed. I settle on top of it, the plush mattress cushioning me. The Frost King watches me through heavy-lidded eyes. He prowls towards me, placing his hands on either side of my hips. I breathe in his scent and feel my nipples harden.

"Stay with me. I want to be with my mate tonight."

A shiver runs through him, and he shakes his head.

"You don't know what you're asking for."

I smile up at him as I slip my shift off my shoulders and let it pool around my waist. The warm air licks over my bare breasts. They are already begging for his touch. I rub my thighs together. Any nerves I have about what I'm asking for are gone. I want this—I need this. I won't allow the curse to prevail without us claiming each other, if only for a night.

Taking his large hand in mine, I settle his cold palm against my heated skin.

"Then show me."

24

———

DOVE

I've never seen the Frost King so unleashed.

His hand tightens on my breast, and before I know it, he's pinned me to the bed beneath his hard body. Lips meet mine in a devastating kiss. His hardness settles against my stomach, setting my blood on fire. My hands go to his back muscles, tracing every groove and contour.

My legs fall to the sides, and he gently slides them between them. His tongue dances with mine while he softly pinches at my nipples. The temperature inside the room is boiling. My heart beats in time with his—we are one in this moment.

The worries that exist beyond the door can't touch us here. There is only us and our shared breaths. He is not a cursed beast, and I am not a human tribute. We are mates, reveling in finding each other after all this time.

Mates, the word is primal yet feels exactly right. From the beginning, I knew how I felt for him wasn't normal—at least not by human standards. He understood me in ways no one else had. My body desired him from the moment we met. Our souls are one, and I can feel them knitting back together in this glorious moment.

"Dove," he groans. "I—I'm trying to be gentle. It's been a long time, and—I've never felt this way about anyone. I don't want to hurt you."

"You won't," I say, kissing him. "Be my first time, Frosty."

He chuckles at the nickname, licking into my mouth with devastating softness. His fingers drift lower, exploring my fevered skin. Skimming over my sides, I gasp into his mouth.

"Ticklish?"

I nod, capturing his lips with mine. His icy fingers stray from my ribs and wrap around the shift bunched at my waist. I lift my hips to help him tug it off me. He tosses it somewhere in the room and hisses when my heated center presses against him.

His mouth leaves mine to explore the expanse of his neck and shoulders. The warm, wet lick of his tongue sends shivers down my spine. Light pours from my necklace, enjoying our coupling almost as much as we are. He nips at my pulse and gently sucks on the skin of my throat. My eyes close, and I give in to sensation.

"Watch me," he commands.

My eyes flutter open as his mouth descends on my chest. He licks over one pert nipple while he molds the other breast in his hand. I arch my back, thrusting them further into his grasp. Pleasure licks along my body and increases the wetness forming between my thighs. A flush breaks out along my chest and cheeks as he releases my nipple with a pop.

"Delicious. My pretty mate is sweet everywhere."

"I—I need more," I pant, the fire inside me raging.

Frosty gives me a knowing smirk before sucking my other nipple into his mouth. I moan as he rolls it between his tongue and teeth. My hands raise to cup his head and hold him to me. All the while, I feel his cool fingers tailing over my stomach in a gentle glide.

I gasp as his hands find my wet center. Firmly, he cups me there, letting me thrust myself against his palm.

"Wet and soft," he groans. "Perfect."

He skims a finger up my slit, teasing my wetness. My legs fall further apart, the muscles aching. His thumb brushes against my clit, and my whole body reacts. I nearly come off the bed at the barest touch.

"I need a taste," he murmurs against me.

I nod my agreement. "Please."

Releasing my breasts, he trails kisses down my middle. His knees hit the side of the bed as he lowers himself to my center. Propping myself up on my elbows, I take in the sight of his white hair and crown nestled between my outstretched thighs. He breathes against my pussy, and I let out a whimper.

"Tell me what you want, Dove."

His icy fingers trail up my inner thighs before hooking underneath them and gently tilting me up and back. I'm bared to his hungry eyes. His chest rises and falls as he breathes me in fully. My face heats again, but I'm not embarrassed. I love the way he looks at me. This only feels right with him—I feel safe.

That knowledge loosens my tongue.

"I want you to taste me."

He groans.

"Where?"

"My pussy." The snowflake hums in agreement and encourages me to be bold. "And then I want to taste you too."

Frosty's eyes blaze as he stares up at me. His hands tighten on the underside of my thighs.

"You'd take me into your sweet mouth?" he purrs. "Taste me with your tongue until I spill down your pretty throat."

"Y—yes," I whimper.

The erotic picture that makes—me before him on my knees while he powers in and out of my waiting mouth—causes more arousal to slide from me. It drips down my thighs and soaks the sheets below me.

I was already on edge. I know it won't take long to reach my peak. His hands find my backside and haul me closer. I grip the sheets to stay upright.

"That will have to wait until another night. I need to be inside your cunt more than my next breath." He throws me a wicked grin. "But first, I need you to come all over my face."

I scream as his mouth lowers on me. Lips and tongues devour me alive. He holds me tight to his face like I'm a feast he can't get enough of. His tongue licks me from top to bottom, even nudging my back entrance, to which I let out a squeal. He sucks my clit into his mouth before swirling his tongue into my entrance.

He alternates between the two to pull every ounce of pleasure from my body. My heart pounds, and a thin sheen of sweat coats me. My fingers thread through his white hair and hold him to me as I grind against his seeking tongue. I watch him slip a cold finger into my entrance. His cool skin heightens my pleasure. It is not long before he slips another inside of me, and I delight in the burning stretch.

Hooking them expertly, my hips wriggle as stars dance behind my eyes. Every muscle grows taut as he sucks my clit. Nipping at it with his blunted fangs, I toss my head back. With one last curl of his fingers, I erupt, shivering and shouting on the bed. I have no concept of the words or names I call him. My body is no longer tethered to this world. I float through my pleasure and land gently on a cloud.

After a moment, I realize my thighs have locked around his head. Spent, I let them fall, noting the indentations of his crown against my inner thighs. His tongue replaces his fingers at my center and eagerly licks up every last drop of my spend. Looking up at me, I shiver at the sight of his mouth smeared with my wetness.

Placing one last gentle kiss on my thigh, he prowls back up my body. Sharing my taste with me, his tongue curls with mine and teases it into submission. He slides us up the bed until my head rests on an overstuffed pillow. With my muscles completely relaxed, I watch through half-lidded eyes as he shucks his pants.

My mouth goes dry at the sight of him. His cock is enormous—not large enough to fear but large enough to know the stretch will be intense. His pale blue shaft is decorated with raised veins that give way to a dark blue head. A bead of moisture leaks from the tip, and I lick my lips.

"Tempting little thing," he groans. "You are mine, Dove."

"Yes," I hiss as he grips his length. I feel his blunt head press against my entrance. "Claim me, my mate."

He howls into my neck as he gently pushes into me. There is a slight pinch, one we both acknowledge with a firm kiss. Slowly, he sheathes himself inside of me until we are flush with each other. The fullness steals my breath. Everything feels right. Golden light wraps around us and fuses us together. This is how we were always meant to be—one.

"Are you okay?" he asks.

His voice is strained and tinged with worry. I nod, cupping his face in my hands.

"Make love to me," I demand. "Fuck me."

With a bruising kiss, he does just that. I feel his hips pull back before they gently push back into me. He is slow with his thrusts at first until I moan into his mouth. That sets him off, and I feel his primal side come out. He powers in and out of me with devastating efficiency. I just reached my peak, and now my body is heading towards another more devastating climax.

My hands fall to his back and roam lower. I cup his backside, urging him to move faster, harder. I meet every brutal thrust he gives me. I raise my hips so that he may spear in deeper. His cock butts up against my womb, and my eyes roll to the back of my head. It's perfect—obscenely so.

"Such a tight cunt," he growls. "You were made for me."

"Yes," I sigh.

"You." *Thrust.* "Are." *Thrust.* "Mine." *Thrust.*

Taking my legs, he tosses them over his shoulders and readjusts his positioning. I'm nearly folded in on myself as he renews his efforts. The position makes everything tighter, and I can feel the veins of his cock dragging inside of me. My wetness aids him in going as deep as possible. He brushes up against a stop inside of me that has my stomach tightening.

"Come on my cock," he demands. "I'm going to flood your pussy with my seed."

"Please! I need it."

"A part of me will always be in you—they can never separate us."

His hands fall to my hips as he holds me in place fucking me with ruthless aggression. It is intense but not painful. Despite his rigorous pounding, there is still a gentleness in how he holds me. His pupils have blown wide, but there is no sign of the beast—only the male I've come to love.

The realization steals my breath and propels me towards my climax. I scream as my body erupts into flames. Every muscle in my body goes taught, and my pussy clamps around his hardness. Frosty snarls, pumping his hips roughly two more times until sheathing himself fully and emptying inside of me. The rush of his warm seeds heightens my pleasure.

My breaths are ragged as he gently removes my legs from his shoulders. His hands come down on either side of my head as he meets my mouth with a gentle kiss. Sweat makes our skin stick together. After a moment, he gently pulls out of me, and a rush of our mingled releases soaks my thighs.

I've never felt more at peace. A sense of belonging and finality settles over me as he wraps me in his arms. Exhaustion weighs on me, but I fight to keep my eyes open. He places lazy kisses against my shoulders, his hands gently skimming up and down my arm.

"How are you?" he asks.

Turning my head, I capture his lips. I should tell him what I feel, but this moment is too perfect for words. In the morning, there will be time for a full declaration. His heart pounds against my shoulder.

Surely, the curse will at least give us another day.

"I'm wonderful."

He smiles against my mouth, but I catch a flash of sadness in his gaze. A coldness seeps from his body that I hadn't noticed before. I narrow my eyes and try to roll over and face him. His lips press a kiss to my temples.

"I will never forget this night," he says, and it sounds like a goodbye.

"What are you—"

But the rest of my sentence never comes as the metallic scent of magic stings my nose. I don't realize what he's done until it's too late. In an instant, I am asleep, drifting through the unending dark.

25

———

THE FROST KING

She is beautiful—his mate.

He thought so from the moment he first laid eyes on her. Barely alive atop that platform, clinging to life yet glowing like a star. He could kill the people of her village for leaving her out there like that. There isn't much time for revenge now. There isn't much time for anything except this.

The final chance to look at her before it all goes dark.

The other half of his soul lays beside him, breathing softly. The one he's waited centuries for. He remembers most of it now—the witch's whispered words. Now that his time has ended, he can at least enjoy his memories once he's frozen. Everything has changed, and yet there is no preventing this. Watching her chest rise and fall, he tucks away the sight of her as the ice creeps in.

Even the beast has gone quiet in supplication, surrendering to their shared fate.

If she was awake, maybe there could be a chance at ending this, but he knows in his heart it is already too late. The ability to be with her—to feel her warmth around him and bask in it

—was one last kindness. He put her to sleep so she wouldn't witness the change.

He'd laugh if the ice wasn't already coating his lungs. It's true—he was never meant to break it. If only they had had more time, but wishing for that would be useless. The ice creeps up fast, consuming his flesh. There is only time now for one final truth to be uttered from his lips.

"I love you, Dove."

His final breath puffs into a cloud of frost against her rosy cheek.

26

DOVE

The cold is what wakes me up.

Someone must've forgotten to stoke the fire.

Opening my eyes, I forget that I'm not in my room. Then, the memories of last night come roaring back as I feel the luxurious soreness in my muscles. My face heats at the pleasure Frosty pulled from my body.

I don't hear him breathing beside me, and the side of the bed feels too cold. Sunlight streams in from the windows. Did he go somewhere? Maybe he's checking on Glimmer. With a start I sit up, remembering my dear friend.

Something heavy pulls against the sheets resting against my chest when I do. Glancing to the side, my whole world shatters in an instant. Denial pierces through me at what I'm seeing. No. No. *No.*

This can't be right—it *can't* be happening.

A scream rips from my lungs as I stare at Frosty's unmoving face. His whole body is ice, like the elves we saw in town. He's curled towards me on the bed. His hands are outstretched as if he can capture me one last time. There is such love radiating from his unseeing eyes.

"Wake up!" I yell. "Please, wake up!"

Heartbreak erupts inside me, and tears spill down my cheeks. Why didn't I tell him I loved him? Why didn't I try harder to break this curse sooner? Now, I have lost him—my mate. He has been stolen from me forever. If I cannot have him and our family I glimpsed at the frozen lake, then I don't want one.

"Don't leave me. I just found you."

My fingers touch his icy skin as sobs wrack my body. I remember every touch and every smile. The kindness he showed me, and the remorse for the male he had been. His heart was changed—how was that not enough to spare him?

I press my forehead against his. He was so alive last night. How could he possibly have turned into—

"He used the last of his magic to save me," a soft voice calls from the corner of the room.

Glimmer buzzes there on her gossamer wings. Her blue skin is rich, and her eyes glow brightly. I glance down at the King and back up to my friend. Tears blur my vision.

"There has to be something—this can't be the end. Not after we only had one night together."

The snow fairy dims, and sadness settles over her features. In the morning light, something is different about Glimmer. Her eyes, which always seemed childlike, are more mature. They regard me with unyielding certainty.

"He would've had more time if he chose not to save me—he would've broken the curse." Glimmer shakes her head. "After all this time, he finally found you, only for it not to matter. I never intended for it to end this way."

My mouth goes dry.

"Glimmer?"

The snow fairy doesn't answer. She merely buzzes towards me on her wings. She glows brightly, nearly scorching my eyes. I watch her glittering form grow and sparkle as she approaches.

Magic dances in the air and swirls around me. Glimmer's small body gives away to another form—her true form.

The light dissipates, and standing before me is a figure I'd recognize anywhere. The sorceress. Her blue eyes sparkle with knowing. She glances at the Frost King, and I want to snarl. It was her curse that made him like this—that robbed us both of our future.

"I know you must be angry with me," she says softly. "Allow me to show you the truth before you do anything rash."

I swallow and stay perfectly still as Glimmer—the sorceress —touches my forehead. I'm sucked down deep into the familiar depths of a memory. The glittering ball from the night the curse was laid comes into view. I stand beside the sorceress as a bound Frost King kneels at our feet. I watch her lean down and press her lips against his ear.

"You will find your mate—oh yes, I see it now," she whispers. "She will be beautiful. Can't you see?"

The second vision I had at the lake swirls around us. My elven self and the Frost King sit on the loveseat surrounded by our child while his hand rests on my stomach. The Frost King's eyes flash, but the sorceress merely chuckles.

"If you succeed in making her fall in love with you, the moment she says the words, all your memories shall return. You will remember the key to setting yourself free. All she needs to do is utter your name, and my curse will be lifted. The name you have blighted with your ignorance and selfishness will be your last hope for salvation." A cruel smile curls her lips. "But she will not be coming for some time, young king. She will be born a human and left to wither in their frozen wastes. You will search the lands for her each year. I hope for your sake that she turns up before five centuries come to pass. If the curse is not broken by then, you will join all the others in their icy prisons."

His skin turns pale, and he sags to the floor.

My heart flops in my chest as I watch her slam the crown down on his head again. Blighting his memory and making the curse impossible to solve. I'm slammed back into my body as I lie beside a frozen Frost King on the bed. Anguish burns through me as I stare up at the sorceress.

"He had to be punished for what he did. *The Crystal Egg* was not just a relic but a conduit of the snow fairies's power. They had suffered once he became king, and as their protector, it was my job to punish him for what he did." Her lips curl down. "But I am not cruel."

I scoff. "You gave him an impossible task."

The sorceress purses her lips.

"Difficult? Yes. Impossible? No." She waves a hand. "I knew he would find you—knew it would happen nearly five centuries after he was cursed. It may seem far-reaching to you, but I was a mother motivated by the love of her children. I had to ensure the one who hurt them was properly dealt with."

"I watched him as Glimmer for centuries. In the beginning, his memories had not yet begun to fade. There was time for him to return to the egg—to ask Glimmer for forgiveness after stealing from her people, but he never did. He only continued treating her like a pest until he forgot why he had disdain for the snow fairies entirely. If he had shown remorse, I would've put you on his path sooner, but it was clear he still had much to learn."

I sigh and look down at Frosty's still form.

"When he finally lost the memory of who he was, I knew there was a chance for him to start over. He befriended Glimmer, all the while ignorant of what he had done. Then he found you, just like I knew he would. When the memories of the past started to reveal themselves to you, I watched him show regret over his actions. He returned the egg and apologized to Glimmer. From how you two looked at each other, I knew he would break the curse in the nick of time."

Her shoulders sag.

"The only thing I didn't see coming was the storm. If he hadn't saved us, I would have perished in Glimmer's body." Blue eyes burn brightly. "You truly changed his heart and turned him into a male worth forgiving—a male who would forsake eternity with his mate to save the smallest member of his kingdom. That is a male worthy of mercy, so I am giving you this final act of kindness."

The sorceress waves a delicate hand, and magic coats my skin. A cold wind causes my ears to ache, and I cry out. Reaching up to touch them, I recoil at the feeling of delicate points. My sight has vastly improved, and I can see myself reflected in the polished stone wall. It is me from the vision—an elf.

"This is how you were always supposed to be. I took great measures to hide you amongst the humans. You've lived countless lives, Dove."

The world around me tilts.

It's as if I can see them play out before me. Sometimes, I was born rich, and sometimes, my family struggled as the one I'm with now does. All of them ended the same way. With me alone until I succumbed to old age. I've been cursed for just as long as Frosty.

"Save your anger and enjoy your future," the sorceress says, touching my cheek. "Say his name and break this curse."

A laugh puffs out of me.

I'm more irate than I ever have been in my life. The rage at what I've just learned—the lives filled with loneliness I've been forced to endure because of this sorceress. All of it boils out of me. My vision blurs with it as I bare my teeth.

"Your curse worked too well, sorceress. He forgot his name long before he ever met me." I huff a humorless laugh. "There's no way for me to break it."

The sorceress's eyes glow.

"Just because he may have forgotten it doesn't mean you never learned it."

"If I hear one more *fucking* riddle, I'm going to—"

A breeze surrounds me, and my snowflake blazes hotly to life. I grip it in my hand to keep it from burning my skin. It pulses against my palm, demanding my attention. The wind around me kicks up again, only this time with a distinct scent of magic.

"*Let us show you,*" a voice whispers in my ear. "*Open your heart to us and feel.*"

Taking a steadying deep breath, I grip the snowflake and let go. Warmth envelopes me in a hug, and I'm shifted into another memory. It swims up from the murky dark as I stand in an empty room save for two marble statues. It is of a male and female, wearing circlets around their heads. Their hands are carved together.

On the floor before them is the Frost King, the silver crown glinting on his head as he pleads at the feet of the statues. Tears run down his cheeks, and my heart gives a painful squeeze.

"Please, mother and father, help guide my mate once I find her. I fear I will have forgotten what I need to do by the time she comes. I have left a clue for her queen's rooms through the hidden passageway. If only you would help guide her to what I've left there—even now, I can't remember. It's all beginning to blur." He shakes his head, and more tears spill over his cheeks. "*The truth is buried deep. When the moon is high, the three stars will guide you to the key.*"

From behind the statues, two figures appear—ghostly and pale. It is his father—the older male from the other memories —and his gorgeous mother. Their matching white hair is long, and their faces are pinched with grief as they stare down at their son. Their eyes lock with mine and glow brightly.

"*See,*" they say in unison.

I am pulled through another memory. This time, it is an

amalgamation of every one I've seen while being here. Only now everything has been revealed to me. That first night I spent in my room, his father's ghost made the rock glow under my window. His mother was urging me down the corridor with a gentle breeze. They summoned the old door and placed the necklace in my path.

They were in the room with egg, looking disappointed in their son. They guided me through the corridor and the storm. His mother had been the one lifting my necklace last night to guide me toward the King to save Glimmer. They were there at every turn.

"Remember what you saw. Save our son," their voices whisper in unison.

I try to shuffle through the memories of everything I've witnessed since getting here—they play over and over in my mind. The first vision, in particular, sticks out. Did his father say his name? I don't think he did. There's something else tickling the edges of my mind. A small wooden chest rests in the corner of the room. It was the same one in the second vision, only that time a sheet had covered it.

When I first glimpsed it, I thought it had been covered in symbols, but as my memory plays it back, I realize it hadn't been symbols at all. It had letters strewn together to make a name.

A name my beloved Frost King taught me to spell.

With a gasp, my eyes fly open. I grasp his frozen face, not caring about the biting cold stinging my skin.

"Jack," I whisper. "Jack, please wake up."

There's a stillness to the room for a moment before everything erupts. Ice cracks from his skin and melts in an instant. The silver crown shakes before splitting in two and sliding from his head. Power pulses against my palms as more cracking echoes around the room.

Finally, his warm, blue skin meets my fingers. A harsh

breath leaves his lungs. Tears flood my eyes as I watch his flare to life before settling on my face. His hands cup the back of my head.

"Dove," he whispers. "My mate—my love."

A sob gets lodged in my throat as I throw myself down on him. His arms wrap around my back as we hold each other on the bed. His hard muscles cradle every one of my soft curves. I sob into his neck. All the anger I felt towards the sorceress melts away, and only happiness and love radiates from me.

I won't let myself get bogged down by thoughts of revenge. Not when I have Frosty—Jack—in my arms and my perfect future laid out before me.

A soft throat clearing has us both looking towards the end of the bed. She looms there, glowing with her unnatural power. Her eyes are severe, but I see a slight curl to her lips.

"You did well, young king. Any lesson worth learning is always difficult."

I glance at Jack, watching a million emotions flood his eyes. His gaze meets mine, and he pulls me deeper into his chest. I get the feeling that we both can't be burdened with thoughts of retribution.

"I've learned my lesson, sorceress. I will be a better king with my mate at my side."

The sorceress's face twists into a grin.

"Excellent," she whispers before disappearing into a glittering breeze of fairy dust.

Jack rises from the bed with me still locked in his arms. Finally alone—and very naked, I'm realizing—the air around us turns heavy. His hand reaches up and traces over the curve of my ear. A delicious shiver runs through me, and Jack smiles.

"There are so many things I want to say to you," he admits. "Paramount among them is that I love you."

Tears burn in my eyes.

"I love you, too."

His mouth finds mine, and it feels like our first kiss. Our souls seal themselves together as our hearts beat as one. His hand slides down my back, groaning as he cups one cheek of my ass in his large palm. A demanding hardness presses against my stomach, and I wiggle against it. He growls into my mouth as his tongue dances with mine.

"Need you," he groans.

I open my mouth to respond when voices begin rising from the hall. Jack sighs before giving me one last squeeze and shifting away.

"All of that will have to wait. Hundreds of confused frost elves are waking up from a five-hundred-year nap that I should attend to."

"That's probably a good idea."

His eyes rove over my naked body. "Once they are handled, you aren't leaving this room for at least a week."

I chuckle and playfully smack at his arm. He pulls me from the bed and lays another devastating kiss on me.

"You should come with me—you're their queen now, after all."

Apprehension threatens to overwhelm me, but it quickly dissipates. There is nothing I can't face when Jack is by my side. My lips curl into a grin.

"Breaking a curse and gaining a royal title in one day?" I shake my head. "Life moves quickly in your kingdom."

"*Our* kingdom," he gently corrects with a wicked grin. "I promise tonight will be deliciously slow as I make up for our lost time together."

A hot shiver runs through me.

"I'll hold you to that, Jack," I say.

Now it is his turn to shiver, his eyes falling shut.

"Say it again."

"Hmm?"

"My name," he pleads. "Say it again."

Reaching up, I place my lips at his ear.

"Jack," I whisper. "Jack."

"You are a devious temptation," he groans. "I need to find you some clothes before I give into my basic nature and fuck you senseless. I promised to be a good king."

"Then we'd better not keep our people waiting."

With a wave of his hand, we are dressed in matching royal apparel. My light blue dress is adorned with a fur trim, highlighting the snowflake around my neck. Jack's pants and shirt are made of the same blue material with a silver thread trim.

He extends his hand towards me, and I grasp it. Together, we take our first step towards our shared future.

27

JACK

This day has been too long.

You'd think I'd have little to complain about after being freshly freed from a centuries-long curse. In truth, my complaints are nothing compared to what I once faced. No beast is laying dormant inside me—the only primal urges I feel are when I glimpse my beautiful mate and wish to ravish her. That can't be helped, especially as I watched her be a gracious and compassionate queen. She easily aided our people by assuaging their concerns and offered answers when she could.

I'll never get over how perfect she is—I thought it from the moment I glimpsed her in the vision shown to me by the sorceress. More importantly, she is kind. For the first time in five hundred years, the thought of the future does not fill me with dread. Instead, I feel light—happy. I am eager to meet each day and show that I have learned from my punishment.

It was harsh—at times unfair—but I made it out with the help of Dove. I will not be drawn back into it. Each day forward takes me further away from my cursed existence until it will all bleed into a distant memory. There is no longer any space in my heart for anger or regrets. The organ seems only to have enough room for loving my mate.

She has saved me, and I'll never stop being grateful for her. The need to show her how important she will always be to me pumps through my veins. Holding the small box, I can feel my parents' proud smiles. They helped her when I needed them to, guiding her through every obstacle so we could end up together like this.

My kingdom is at rest as the blue moon shines above. In the coming days, I anticipate many questions my people will have about the centuries they've been asleep. For now, everything is quiet, and the only question I'm concerned about is the very serious one I'm about to pose to Dove.

Tucking the small box into my pocket, it seems to weigh a hundred pounds as I travel from the castle's bowels up to the king's rooms. I never stayed in them as a prince—the memory of my father clung to the walls.

Now, I have claimed them for Dove and myself. My magic has been restored, and I transformed the room into one where we can spend every morning waking up together and each night wrapped around the other. Our future will be solidified inside that room. My blood heats in anticipation.

All day, I have managed to keep my hands off her. A feat a weaker male would have succumbed to. After watching her sway on her feet in the front room, I sent her to rest a few hours ago. Exhaustion had etched itself on her lovely face. My only hope is that she's rested enough for what I have planned for her.

After the sorceress returned her to her true elven form, she is now as immortal as I am. Our life together will be endless, sprawling into centuries. I want her tied to me in every way—to leave no uncertainty that she is mine in the minds of anyone.

The thought quickens my steps as I take them two at a time. Rushing down the hallway, I open the doors to our room and am immediately drawn to her. Clad only in a simple silk nightgown, I watch her nipples pebble against the front of it. Her eyes find mine as she gently glides a brush through her long, dark tresses. Mischief tips her lips upwards.

I pause at the entryway, my mouth going dry. Was there ever a male as lucky as I?

"Are you done being king for the evening?" she asks softly.

All the blood in my body races towards my cock.

"Yes," I respond. "Now, I am merely a male. One is who is utterly obsessed with his mate."

Her laugh tickles my skin and draws me closer. I watch her set the brush down beside her. The dark wave of her silken hair falls down her back. The nightgown she wears is barely more than a strip of blue fabric. Her creamy pale skin glows in the dim light.

She raises a brow.

"You look like you want to ask me something."

Dove reads me so easily, though I suppose my intent is obvious. Every muscle in my body is tense as I kneel before her. Staring up at her glowing face, I lick my lips and try to find the perfect words to convey what I wish to ask.

I am far too eager of a male because instead of speaking, my errant hands dig into my pocket and produce the small velvet box. Flipping open the top, Dove's gasp is music to my ears as she takes in the ring. It is a simple silver band adorned with sapphires and diamonds. She looks at me, her mouth slightly open.

"I know it's fast," I say. "We still have much to learn about each other, but I want you to wear my ring as we do. I want everyone to know you are mind just as I am yours."

Dove laughs, tears brimming in her dark eyes.

"A mate, a kingdom, and a marriage proposal. What more could today bring? A baby?"

My grin widens. She isn't pregnant, not yet, at least.

"Soon, you will grow round with our child. I will happily keep trying until you do."

Her delicate foot playfully pushes against my chest.

"You are incorrigible," she giggles. "But I love you all the same. I want to marry you, Jack. I never want us to be apart."

Her eyes soften.

"And I want my family brought here from our village at once."

I nod. "I have already sent males and horses to retrieve them."

Tears rim her wide eyes, and she holds her hand towards me. I gently take it and slide the ring onto her slender finger. It sparkles brilliantly. Placing a kiss on her hand, she sighs as I press another one along her wrist. My mouth travels upward, tasting every inch of her delicious skin.

She shivers as I get to her neck, biting and sucking along her delicate flesh. Her sweet scent invades my nostrils and coats my tongue. Her hands fall to my shoulders, encouraging me with her soft moans to keep going. My mouth travels higher to find hers. Once our lips touch, all gentleness is lost.

It is a fight to dominate the other's mouth. I revel in her submission as her tongue tangles with mine. Her small hand palms me over my pants, and I snarl against her. Breaking the kiss, she stares up at me with wild eyes.

"You said I could taste you the next time," she reminds me.

"Dove," I growl as she slides to the floor.

Her hands go to the thin straps of her nightgown and lower them. The silk pools around her waist as her breasts are bared. Her pink nipples are hard and beg for my mouth. If there wasn't so much determination in her gaze, I'd gladly be on my knees before her.

If my mate wants me in her mouth, who am I to deny her?

She licks her lips before unbuttoning my pants. The pool around my ankles as my length juts out towards her. A gasp escapes her lips as she gently grips me. I could spend from the slight touch alone. Her pupils are blown wide as she stares up at me. The sight of her face partially obscured by my cock causes my heart to race.

"Tell me what to do," she whispers.

Her hand glides along me from root to tip. I grit my teeth against the need rushing through me.

"That," I groan. "Do that a bit harder."

She pumps me roughly in her small. A bead of my seed leaks out from the tip. She stares at it transfixed before darting her pink tongue to catch it. Swallowing it down, she shivers at the taste. I can smell the delicious state of her pussy. She's already wet for me.

"Take me into your mouth," I urge. "Use your tongue—like when we kiss."

Dove lowers her dark head and opens her mouth. Placing the blunt head of my cock on her tongue, I pulse with need as she gently tastes it. A moan vibrates from her throat, and the grip on my control slips.

Slowly, I move my hips forward, sheathing more of myself inside her hot, wet mouth. She groans, continuing to pump me with her hand as she takes me deeper. She licks over the veins of my cock and swirls her tongue around the tip. The seed leaking from me is quickly sucked down as her mouth makes slippery sounds along my hardness.

Her eagerness makes my head spin. To know I am the first and only male to have her like this sends a primal urge rushing through me. My hands spear through her dark hair, anchoring her mouth open as I use my hips to thrust along her tongue.

Saliva pours down my shaft as she continues to suck me. I hit the back of her throat, and she gags, her eyes watering. Pulling out, I open my mouth to apologize, but her brilliant smile stops me.

"More," she demands. "Harder."

Holding her head in my hands, I grin at her.

"Whatever you want."

I unleash myself on her mouth. Thrusting my hips in quick succession, she meets each one with her tongue. It would seem that she's a fast learner in all things. Her hand drifts lower to cup and massage me while she never loses her rhythm. Teeth gently scrape my length, and my blood turns to fire. If I'm not careful, I'll spend down her throat and not in her perfect pussy.

Soon, I'll feed her my seed, but not tonight. I need to watch it seep out of her little cunt and soak the bed below her. The sight is seared into my memory, and I need to see it again. I pull her from my cock, and she gives a high-pitched protest. Saliva and come are smeared around her mouth as I kiss her soundly. Without a word, I toss her onto the bed.

Hefting her hips into my hands, I raise her on all fours before kneeling behind her at the center of the bed. My mouth lowers to her soaking wet pussy. I spear my tongue into her, delighting in her squeal of pleasure. I lick and suck her, tasting how much she enjoyed having her mouth on my cock.

She tastes sweeter than any wine.

Needing to feel her wrapped around me, I remove my mouth and guide my cock to her entrance. I drag it along her wetness, coating myself before gently pressing into her.

"Jack," she sighs.

My name on her lips makes my body tighten.

"Tell me what you want," I command.

She looks over her shoulder at me. Her smile is wanton, but her eyes swim with love and adoration. Our souls are one—as are our hearts. When we are joined like this, they return together. I match her look of love with one of my own. She shivers and grips the sheets in her hands.

"Fuck me, Jack. Come inside of me. I want to feel it."

With a snarl, I give my mate what she wants. My hands grip her waist as I retreat my hips and slam into her. The force nearly knocks her off balance, but I keep her upright. I power into her again and again as her moans echo around us. Her spine bows in supplication to my dominance. Her pussy grips me like a fist, sucking me further into her.

"My mate's pussy is perfect," I snarl. "If only you could see how greedy it is—tightening on me like a good girl."

"Jack," she sighs. "Please. More."

Her hands slide on the bed, and she lowers her head. Incoherent moans and whimpers leave her lips. She works herself back on me, allowing me to go deeper. The soft globes of her ass absorb the impact of my thrusts. Lifting my hand, I trace the seam of her backside, dipping into the untouched hole and delighting in her squeal.

"Soon," I vow. "My seed will seep from here as well."

Her breathing is ragged. A pink flush spills from her cheeks down her chest. Sweat makes her pale skin glimmer.

"Jack," she pants. "I'm close."

Her tightening on my cock makes me renew my efforts. I slip my hand from her ass and drag it around to her front. Finding her needy clit, I rub tight circles on it. Her mouth opens with a silent scream, and her hips freeze. Her pussy clamps down on me, and I come with a roar. My body locks up as I spill deep inside of her waiting heat.

When I am finally spent, and she sags to the bed before me, I gently withdraw. Sticky release flows from her little pussy and trails down her thighs. Dove falls to the bed in a graceless heap. I chuckle, laying beside her and tucking her into my side. Shaking with waves of pleasure, heavy breaths pass from her lips.

I tuck a piece of hair away from her sweaty brow. Her eyes stare up at me, still coming down from her climax.

Yesterday, I was a cursed male. Today, I am blessed beyond my wildest dreams. With Dove in my arms and by my side, the cruel male I was was long gone. For her, I will be better. Every day, I will prove myself worthy of her and the gift I have been given.

I press a kiss to her swollen lips.

"Mmm," she hums. "How can I still want more of you? My limbs feel like jam."

I chuckle, rolling on top of her to take her mouth fully. Moaning against me, she raises her hips, soaking me with our mingling releases. My lips find her breasts and tease each nipple into a harsh peak. Her hands go to my hair as I trail lower down her body.

"Again?" she asks as my lips hover over her center.

I cup her behind her knees and push her up and back, baring her pussy to my waiting mouth.

"Again."

EPILOGUE

DOVE - TWENTY YEARS LATER

The castle smells like Mama's famous cinnamon bread. I press a hand to my round stomach as it growls. A smile plays on my lips. I've been craving it for weeks since Jack and I discovered we were having a little female. She sleeps as I sit in the library, finishing one of my latest novels. A stack of books rests atop the table next to me. I set down the novel in my hands. My eyes are beginning to ache. The low fire tells me I've been here for quite some time.

The door to the library peels open, revealing my handsome mate and husband. Wearing simple wool clothes and a dark traveling cloak, a silver circlet rests on his brow. His leather boots squeak on the tile floor as he approaches me. His eyes turn my blood hot. Warmth blooms in my chest.

This pregnancy has made me more insatiable for him than ever.

He has spent many days away at the fairy fortress, attending to their needs as a good king should. Today, he returned home early, and I could not be more grateful. He comes to my side, pressing a kiss to my temple and resting his warm hand on my growing stomach.

"How are you, my lovely mate?" His blue eyes sparkle. "How is our little one?"

"Resting, thankfully. She is quite active during the morning."

Jack nods, brushing snow from his cape before hanging it before the fire.

"How are the snow fairies?" I inquire. "Are the bears giving them any more trouble?"

Jack shakes his head, settling onto the seat next to me. He tucks me into his side, and I nuzzle into him.

"I've implemented new protection wards for them. Nothing should be able to get through."

I nod.

"I only wish I could accompany you. As queen, we are supposed to be a united front for our people."

"You need your rest. She'll be here before we know it." His lips skim over my cheek as his hands trail up and down my arms. "Speaking of, we still need to decide on a name for her."

"The older ones are already named after you," I remind him. "Jacks and Jackson—we are dreadfully uncreative."

Jack laughs. It is a family tradition to name all males after their father, and though I'd love for us to have a dozen children, I fear we've already run out of variations for Jack.

Dove, on the other hand...

"It is only fair that I get to name her," I say.

"Whatever my mate wants, she shall have. Always."

I hum in my throat.

"All I want right now is a piece of cinnamon bread."

"Ask, and you shall receive," a warm voice calls from the library's opening.

Turning in the loveseat, I see Mama's gray-streaked hair and a steaming loaf of cinnamon bread in her hands. My mouth waters and Mama quickly walks over to me. I attempt to rise to greet her, but she urges me to sit still. Kissing my forehead, she slices into the bread.

"You need to keep up your strength so my granddaughter can continue to grow strong."

She settles a sugary slice on a ceramic plate and hands it to me. Steam rolls off the crust, and I blow on it to cool it faster. Satisfied that it won't burn me, I take a bite and moan at the sweet and spicy flavor. It is soft and crunchy at the same time.

She sells dozens of loaves daily out of her bakery in town. Once she and Sophia arrived at the castle, Mama found her calling, using her baking skills to bring others in the town joy. When Jack's males came to collect her, Mama told me no one noticed. They were too busy watching the snow that had plagued them for centuries melt away.

Our time in Snowdale feels like a different lifetime. Nothing is tying us to it now. Jon Nine-Fingers never asked after me once I was taken at *the Offering*. Mama says he died on a hunting expedition a few days after Jack took me. I couldn't find it in me to be sad.

Life has been simple here. It took a while to adjust to being queen, and it took our people time to see Jack for the man he was, not who he had been. He still has amends to make, but he strives to improve each day.

We love each other and the family we've built with everything we have. After living through so much pain and heartache, we owe it to ourselves to enjoy each moment. What is life without love? I wouldn't know—there is so much of it here I wonder if we will all drown in it one day.

A flurry of movement at the door catches my eye. I watch our other two children appear—our eldest, with his dark hair and sparkling blue eyes. Then, there is our soon-to-be middle child. With his curling white hair, he looks especially like his father today.

"We smelled cinnamon," Jackson announces, claiming a

plate of bread while Mama kisses his fair head. Jacks follows suit, devouring his slice in an instant.

"Save some for your aunt and uncle," I gently remind them.

As if my words summoned them, Sophia appears with her elven husband at her side. Their matching blue eyes sparkle as they walk into the living room. Plume had met my sister when he came to work in Mama's bakery. One thing had led to another, and well—their beautiful halfling daughter, Emmeline, floats into the library behind them.

Everyone takes a slice of the excellent bread, and my heart fills with joy. It overflows and spills from me. Tears prick my eyes as I look up at my mate—my everything.

"Thank you for choosing me," I whisper so only he can hear. "My life is the better for it. There would be none of this without you."

Sparkling tears glimmer in his eyes as he brushes a kiss against me.

"Thank you for breaking the curse—for seeing the male I could be and loving me through all of it. Without you, I'd have nothing."

My hand rests on my stomach as I take in my family. Love wraps around each of us—tethering us with its golden thread.

"Together, we have everything," I declare. "Forever."

His hand settles atop mine, and I breathe in his pine scent.

"Forever," he agrees.

Warmth pours from his body and into me. Our souls knit together, and I feel the completion only he can give me.

Our ever-lasting love is more powerful than any curse.

READ MY OTHER SERIES

Interconnected monster romance standalone on Kindle Unlimited!

Short and spicy monster romance novellas following a different diabolical looking creature!

ACKNOWLEDGMENTS

Thank you all so much to my dedicated readers! None of this would be possible without you. I can't wait for you all to join me in the next one.

xoxo Charlotte

ABOUT THE AUTHOR

Charlotte Swan is twenty-six year old, living in Chicago. When she is not dreaming about being whisked away to a world filled with magic and sexy monsters, she is busy being a freelance social media marketer and full-time smut lover. To read her debut novel *Taken by the Dark Elf King*, hear about her upcoming projects, or to connect with her on social media please find her on her website or by scanning the code below.

www.authorcharlotteswan.com